A

COLLECTION

OF

FAMILIAR QUOTATIONS

by

JOHN BARTLETT

THE WISDOM LIBRARY

A DIVISION OF

PHILOSOPHICAL LIBRARY

New York

PN6081 B 27

Distributed to the trade by
Citadel Press, Inc.
A subsidiary of Lyle Stuart, Inc.
120 Enterprise Ave., Secaucus, N.J. 07094
ISBN 0–8065–0250–9

TEMPEST

There's nothing ill can dwell in such a temple:
If the ill spirit have so fair a house,
Good things will strive to dwell with 't.   Act i. Sc. 2.

I will be correspondent to command,
And do my spiriting gently.   Act i. Sc. 2.

A very ancient and fish-like smell.   Act ii. Sc. 2.

Misery acquaints a man with strange bedfellows.
                                                Act ii. Sc. 2.

Our revels now are ended: these our actors,
As I foretold you, were all spirits, and
Are melted into air, into thin air:
And, like the baseless fabric of this vision,
The cloud-capped towers, the gorgeous palaces,
The solemn temples, the great globe itself,
Yea, all which it inherit, shall dissolve,
And, like an insubstantial pageant faded,
Leave not a rack behind.   Act iv. Sc. 1.

          We are such stuff
As dreams are made of, and our little life
Is rounded with a sleep.   Act iv. Sc. 1.

TWO GENTLEMEN OF VERONA

I have no other but a woman's reason;
I think him so, because I think him so.   Act i. Sc. 2.
To make a virtue of necessity.   Act iv. Sc. 1.
Is she not passing fair?   Act iv. Sc. 4.

MERRY WIVES OF WINDSOR

Faith, thou hast some crotchets in thy head now.
                                                Act ii. Sc. 1.

1

Why, then the world's mine oyster,
Which I with sword will open.   Act ii. Sc. 2.
They say, there is divinity in odd numbers, either in
nativity, chance, or death.   Act v. Sc. 1.

TWELFTH NIGHT

If music be the food of love, play on,
Give me excess of it; that, surfeiting,
The appetite may sicken, and so die. —
That strain again; — it had a dying fall;
O, it came o'er my ear like the sweet south,
That breathes upon a bank of violets,
Stealing and giving odor.   Act i. Sc. 1.
I am sure care 's an enemy to life.   Act i. Sc. 3.
'T is beauty truly blent, whose red and white
Nature's own sweet and cunning hand laid on.
          Act i. Sc. 5.
Dost thou think, because thou art virtuous, there shall
be no more cakes and ale?   Act ii. Sc. 3.
          She never told her love,
But let concealment, like a worm in the bud,
Feed on her damask cheek: she pined in thought,
And, with a green and yellow melancholy,
She sat, like Patience on a monument,
Smiling at grief.   Act ii. Sc. 4.
Oh, what a deal of scorn looks beautiful
In the contempt and anger of his lip!   Act iii. Sc. 1.
Love sought is good, but given unsought is better.
          Act iii. Sc. 1.
Let there be gall enough in thy ink; though thou write
with a goose-pen, no matter.   Act iii. Sc. 2.
Some are born great, some achieve greatness, and some
have greatness thrust upon them.   Act iii. Sc. 4.

MEASURE FOR MEASURE

          Spirits are not finely touched
But to fine issues.   Act i. Sc. 1.
          Our doubts are traitors,
And make us lose the good we oft might win,
By fearing to attempt.   Act i. Sc. 5.

                    O, it is excellent
To have a giant's strength; but it is tyrannous
To use it like a giant.   Act ii. Sc. 2.
                    But man, proud man!
Drest in a little brief authority,

       .   .   .   .   .   .

Plays such fantastic tricks before high Heaven
As make the angels weep.   Act ii. Sc. 2.
The miserable have no other medicine,
But only hope.   Act iii. Sc. 1.
The sense of death is most in apprehension;
And the poor beetle that we tread upon
In corporal sufferance finds a pang as great
As when a giant dies.   Act iii. Sc. 1.
Ay, but to die, and go we know not where;
To lie in cold obstruction, and to rot.   Act iii. Sc. 1.
          Take, O take those lips away,
              That so sweetly were forsworn;
          And those eyes, the break of day,
              Lights that do mislead the morn;
          But my kisses bring again,
              Seals of love, but sealed in vain.*

MUCH ADO ABOUT NOTHING

He hath indeed better bettered expectation.
                                        Act i. Sc. 1.
Friendship is constant in all other things,
Save in the office and affairs of love.

-----

   * This song is found in "The Bloody Brother, or Rollo, Duke
of Normandy," by Beaumont and Fletcher, Act 5, Sc. 2, with
the following additional stanza: —
              "Hide, O hide those hills of snow,
                  Which thy frozen bosom bears,
              On whose tops the fruits that grow
                  Are of those that April wears;
              But first set my poor heart free,
                  Bound in those icy chains for thee."
There has been much controversy about the authorship, but
the more probable opinion seems to be that the second stanza
was added by Fletcher.

Therefore, all hearts in love use their own tongues;
Let every eye negotiate for itself,
And trust no other agent.
Act ii. Sc. 1.
Silence is the perfectest herald of joy; I were but little
happy, if I could say how much.   Act ii. Sc. 1.
Sits the wind in that corner?   Act ii. Sc. 3.
When I said I should die a bachelor, I did not think I
should live till I were married.   Act iii. Sc. 1.
Some, Cupid kills with arrows, some with traps.
Act iii. Sc. 1.
Every one can master a grief, but he that hath it.
Act iii. Sc. 2.
Are you good men and true?   Act iii. Sc. 3.
Is most tolerable, and not to be endured.   Act iii. Sc. 3.
Comparisons are odorous.   Act iii. Sc. 4.
O that he were here to write me down — an ass!
Act iv. Sc. 2.
A fellow that had losses.   Act iv. Sc. 2.
For there was never yet philosopher
That could endure the toothache patiently.
Act v. Sc. 1.

MIDSUMMER NIGHT'S DREAM

But earthly happier is the rose distilled
Than that which, withering on the virgin thorn,
Grows, lives, and dies in single blessedness.
Act i. Sc. 1.
Ah me! for aught that ever I could read,
Could ever hear by tale or history,
The course of true love never did run smooth.
Act i. Sc. 1.
Love looks not with the eyes, but with the mind;
And therefore is winged Cupid painted blind.
Act i. Sc. 1.
A proper man as any one shall see in a summer's day.
Act i. Sc. 2.
In maiden meditation, fancy free.   Act ii. Sc. 2.
I'll put a girdle round about the earth
In forty minutes.   Act ii. Sc. 2.
I know a bank whereon the wild thyme blows,

Where ox-lips and the nodding violet grows.
Act ii. Sc. 2.

So we grew together,
Like to a double cherry, seeming parted.
Act iii. Sc. 2.

The poet's eye, in a fine frenzy rolling,
Doth glance from heaven to earth, from earth to heaven,
And as imagination bodies forth
The forms of things unknown, the poet's pen
Turns them to shape, and gives to airy nothing
A local habitation and a name.   Act v. Sc. 1.

LOVE'S LABOR'S LOST

A Merrier Man

Within the limit of becoming mirth,
I never spent an hour's talk withal.   Act ii. Sc. 1.
He draweth the thread of his verbosity finer than the
staple of his argument.   Act v. Sc. 1.

MERCHANT OF VENICE

I hold the world but as the world, Gratiano;
A stage, where every man must play a part,
And mine a sad one.   Act i. Sc. 1.
Why should a man, whose blood is warm within,
Sit like his grandsire cut in alabaster?   Act i. Sc. 1.

I am Sir Oracle,
And when I ope my lips, let no dog bark!   Act i. Sc. 1.
Gratiano speaks an infinite deal of nothing; more than
any man in all Venice. His reasons are as two grains of
wheat hid in two bushels of chaff: you shall seek all day
ere you find them: and, when you have them, they are not
worth the search.   Act i. Sc. 1.
Even there, where merchants most do congregate.
Act i. Sc. 3.

The Devil can cite Scripture for his purpose.
Act i. Sc. 3.

Sufferance is the badge of all our tribe.   Act i. Sc. 3.

Many a time, and oft,
On the Rialto, have you rated me.
Act i. Sc. 3.

It is a wise father that knows his own child.

Act ii. Sc. 2.

All things that are,
Are with more spirits chased than enjoyed.

Act ii. Sc. 6.

All that glitters is not gold.   Act ii. Sc. 7.

I am a Jew: hath not a Jew eyes? hath not a Jew hands, organs, dimensions, senses, affections, passions?

Act iii. Sc. 1.

Thus when I shun Scylla, your father, I fall into Charybdis, your mother.   Act iii. Sc. 5.

What! wouldst thou have a serpent sting thee twice?

Act iv. Sc. 1.

The quality of mercy is not strained;
It droppeth, as the gentle rain from heaven
Upon the place beneath: it is twice blessed;
It blesseth him that gives, and him that takes.

Act iv. Sc. 1.

A Daniel come to judgment.   Act iv. Sc. 1.

Is it so nominated in the bond.   Act iv. Sc. 1.

.   .   .   .   .   .

I cannot find it; 't is not in the bond?   Act iv. Sc. 1.

I have thee on the hip.   Act iv. Sc. 1.

I thank thee, Jew, for teaching me that word.

Act v. Sc. 1.

How sweet the moonlight sleeps upon this bank!

Act v. Sc. 1.

I am never merry when I hear sweet music.

Act v. Sc. I.

The man that hath no music in himself,
Nor is not moved with concord of sweet sounds,
Is fit for treasons, stratagems, and spoils.
How far that little candle throws his beams!
So shines a good deed in a naughty world. Act v. Sc. 1.

AS YOU LIKE IT

We said: that was laid on with a trowel.   Act i. Sc. 2.

My pride fell with my fortunes.   Act i. Sc. 2.

Cel. Not a word?
Ros. Not one to throw at a dog.

Act i. S. 3.

O how full of briers is this working-day world!
Act i. Sc. 3.
Sweet are the uses of adversity,
Which, like the toad, ugly and venomous,
Wears yet a precious jewel in his head. Act ii. Sc. 1.
And this our life, exempt from public haunts,
Finds tongues in trees, books in the running brooks,
Sermons in stones, and good in everything. Act ii. Sc. 1.
"Poor deer," quoth he, "thou mak'st a testament,
As wordlings do, giving thy sum of more
To that which had too much." Act ii. Sc. 1.
And He that doth the ravens feed,
Yea, providently caters for the sparrow,
Be comfort to my age! Act ii. Sc. 3.
For in my youth I never did apply
Hot and rebellious liquors in my blood;

.   .   .   .   .   .

Therefore my age is as a lusty winter,
Frosty, but kindly. Act ii. Sc. 3.
And railed on lady Fortune in good terms,
In good set terms. . . . . .
And looking on it with lack-lustre eye,

.   .   .   .   .   .

"Thus we may see," quoth he, "how the world wags.

.   .   .   .   .   .

And so from hour to hour we ripe and ripe,
And then from hour to hour we rot and rot,
And thereby hangs a tale."

.   .   .   .   .   .

Motley 's the only wear.
If ladies be but young and fair,
They have the gift to know it. Act ii. Sc. 7.
I must have liberty
Withal, as large a charter as the wind,
To blow on whom I please. Act ii. Sc. 7.
The *why* is plain as way to parish church Act ii. Sc. 7.
All the world's a stage
And all the men and women merely players:
They have their exits and their entrances,
And one man in his time plays many parts.

.   .   .   .   .   .

And then, the whining school-boy, with his satchel,

And shining morning face, creeping like snail
Unwillingly to school. And then, the lover,
Sighing like furnace, with a woful ballad
Made to his mistress' eyebrow. Then, a soldier,
Full of strange oaths, and bearded like the pard,
Jealous in honor, sudden and quick in quarrel,
Seeking the bubble reputation
Even in the cannon's mouth. And then the justice,

.   .   .   .   .   .

Full of wise saws and modern instances,
And so he plays his part. The sixth age shifts
Into the lean and slippered pantaloon.

.   .   .   .   .

Last scene of all,
That ends this strange, eventful history,
Is second childishness, and mere oblivion.

Act ii. Sc. 7.

Blow, blow, thou winter wind,
Thou art not so unkind
As man's ingratitude.

Act ii. Sc. 7.

Hast any philosophy in thee, shepherd?   Act iii. Sc. 2.
Truly, I would the gods had made thee poetical.

Act iii. Sc. 3.

I had rather have a fool to make me merry, than experience to make me sad.   Act iv. Sc. 1.
Men have died from time to time, and worms have
eaten them, but not for love.   Act iv. Sc. 1.

Pacing through the forest,
Chewing the food of sweet and bitter fancy.

Act iv. Sc. 3.

How bitter a thing it is to look into happiness through
another man's eyes!   Act v. Sc. 2.
Your *If* is the only peacemaker; much virtue in *If*.

Act v. Sc. 4.

EPILOGUE

Good wine needs no bush.

TAMING OF THE SHREW

And thereby hangs a tale.   Act iv. Sc. 1.

My cake is dough.   Act v. Sc. 2.

WINTER'S TALE

A merry heart goes all the day,
Your sad tires in a mile-a.
                                           Act iv. Sc. 2.
              Daffodils,
That come before the swallow dares, and take
The winds of March with beauty; violets, dim,
But sweeter than the lids of Juno's eyes,
Or Cytherea's breath.   Act iv. Sc. 3.
              When you do dance, I wish you
A wave o' the sea, that you might ever do
Nothing but that.   Act iv. Sc. 3.

ALL'S WELL THAT ENDS WELL

              It were all one,
That I should love a bright, particular star,
And think to wed it, he is so above me.
                                           Act i. Sc. 1.

              Praising what is lost
Makes the remembrance dear.   Act v. Sc. 3.

COMEDY OF ERRORS

They brought one Pinch, a hungry, lean-faced villain,
A mere anatomy.   Act v. Sc. 1.

MACBETH

When shall we three meet again,
In thunder, lightning, or in rain?   Act i. Sc. 1.
Fair is foul, and foul is fair.   Act i. Sc. 1.
The earth hath bubbles, as the water has,
And these are of them.   Act i. Sc. 3.
              Two truths are told,
As happy prologues to the swelling act
Of the imperial theme.   Act i. Sc. 3.
              Present fears
Are less than horrible imaginings.   Act i. Sc. 3.
              Come what come may,

Time and the hour runs through the roughest day.
                                              Act i. Sc. 3.

           Nothing in his life
Became him like the leaving it.   Act i. Sc. 4.

           There 's no art
To find the mind's construction in the face.   Act i. Sc. 4.

           Yet I do fear thy nature;
It is too full of the milk of human kindness
To catch the nearest way.   Act i. Sc. 5.

Your face, my thane, is as a book, where men
May read strange matters.   Act i. Sc. 5.

If it were done, when 't is done, then 't were well
It were done quickly.   Act i. Sc. 7.

           That but this blow
Might be the be-all and the end-all here.   Act i. Sc. 7.

           This even-handed justice
Commends the ingredients of our poisoned chalice
To our own lips.   Act i. Sc. 7.

           Besides, this Duncan
Hath borne his faculties so meek, hath been
So clear in his great office, that his virtues
Will plead like angels, trumpet-tongued, against
The deep damnation of his taking off.
                                              Act i. Sc. 7.

           I have no spur
To prick the sides of my intent, but only
Vaulting ambition, which o'erleaps itself,
And falls on the other——   Act i. Sc. 7.

           I have bought
Golden opinions from all sorts of people.
                                              Act i. Sc. 7.

Letting *I dare not* wait upon *I would,*
Like the poor cat i' the adage.   Act i. Sc. 7.

I dare do all that may become a man;
Who dares do more, is none.   Act i. Sc. 7.

But screw your courage to the sticking-place.
                                              Act i. Sc. 7.

Is this a dagger which I see before me,
The handle towards my hand?   Act ii. Sc. 1.

Thou sure and firm-set earth,
Hear not my steps, which way they walk, for fear
The very stones prate of my whereabout.

Act ii. Sc. 1.

For it is a knell
That summons thee to heaven or to hell!   *Act ii. Sc. 1.*

The attempt, and not the deed,
Confound us.   *Act ii. Sc. 2.*
Sleep, that knits up the ravelled sleave of care.

Act ii. Sc. 2.

Infirm of purpose!   *Act ii. Sc. 2.*
The labor we delight in, physics pain.   *Act ii. Sc. 3.*
The wine of life is drawn, and the mere lees
Is left this vault to brag of.   *Act ii. Sc. 3.*
A falcon, towering in her pride of place,
Was by a mousing owl hawked at, and killed.

Act ii. Sc. 4.

Upon my head they placed a fruitless crown,
And put a barren sceptre in my gripe,
Thence to be wrenched with an unlineal hand,
No son of mine succeeding.   *Act iii. Sc. 1.*
Mur. We are men, my liege.
Mac. Ay, in the catalogue ye go for men.

Act iii. Sc. 1.

We have scotched the snake, not killed it.   *Act iii. Sc. 2.*

Duncan is in his grave!
After life's fitful fever he sleeps well.   *Act iii. Sc. 2.*
But now, I am cabined, cribbed, confined, bound in
To saucy doubts and fears.   *Act iii. Sc. 4.*
Now good digestion wait on appetite,
And health on both!   *Act iii. Sc. 4.*
Thou canst not say, I did it: never shake
Thy gory locks at me.   *Act iii. Sc. 4.*
Thou hast no speculation in those eyes
Which thou dost glare with!   *Act iii. Sc. 4.*
What man dare, I dare.   *Act iii. Sc. 4.*
Take any shape but that, and my firm nerves
Shall never tremble.   *Act iii. Sc. 4.*
Stand not upon the order of your going,
But go at once.   *Act iii. Sc. 4.*

Can such things be,
And overcome us like a summer's cloud,
Without our special wonder?   *Act iii. Sc. 4.*

Black spirits and white,
Red spirits and gray,
Mingle, mingle, mingle,
You that mingle may.*

Act iv. Sc. 1.

By the pricking of my thumbs,
Something wicked this way comes.   Act iv. Sc. 1.
A deed without a name.   Act iv. Sc. 1.
          I'll make assurance double sure,
And take a bond of fate.   Act iv. Sc. 1.
Show his eyes, and grieve his heart!
Come like shadows, so depart.   Act iv. Sc. 1.
What! will the line stretch out of the crack of doom?

Act iv. Sc. 1.

The flighty purpose never is o'ertook,
Unless the deed go with it.   Act iv. Sc. 1.
What, all my pretty chickens, and their dam,
At one fell swoop?   Act iv. Sc. 3.
I cannot but remember such things were,
That were most precious to me.   Act iv. Sc. 3.
O, I could play the woman with mine eyes,
And braggart with my tongue!   Act iv. Sc. 3.
          My way of life
Is fallen into the sear, the yellow leaf;
And that which should accompany old age,
As honor, love, obedience, troops of friends,
I must not look to have; but, in their stead,
Curses, not loud, but deep, mouth-honor, breath,
Which the poor heart would fain deny, but dare not.

Act v. Sc. 3.

          Not so sick, my lord,
As she is troubled with thick-coming fancies,
That keep her from her rest.   Act v. Sc. 3.
Canst thou not minister to a mind diseased;
Pluck from the memory a rooted sorrow;
Raze out the written troubles of the brain;
And, with some sweet oblivious antidote,
Cleanse the stuffed bosom of that perilous stuff

---

* These lines occur also in "The Witch" of Thomas Middleton,
Act 5, Sc. 2; and it is uncertain to which the priority should be
ascribed.

Which weighs upon the heart?   Act v. Sc. 3.
Throw physic to the dogs: I'll none of it.   Act v. Sc. 3.
I would applaud thee to the very echo,
That should applaud again.   Act v. Sc. 3.
Hang out our banners on the outward walls;
The cry is still, *They come.*   Act v. Sc. 5.
To-morrow, and to-morrow, and to-morrow,
Creeps in this petty pace from day to day,
To the last syllable of recorded time;
And all our yesterdays have lighted fools
The way to dusty death. Out, out, brief candle!
Life's but a walking shadow; a poor player,
That struts and frets his hour upon the stage,
And then is heard no more; it is a tale
Told by an idiot, full of sound and fury,
Signifying nothing.   Act v. Sc. 5.
            Blow, wind! come, wrack!
At least we'll die with harness on our back.
                                                Act v. Sc. 5.
I bear a charmed life.   Act v. Sc. 7.
That keep the word of promise to our ear,
And break it to our hope.   Act v. Sc. 7.
            Lay on, Macduff;
And damned be him that first cries, Hold, enough!
                                                Act v. Sc. 7.

KING JOHN

For courage mounteth with occasion.   Act ii. Sc. 1.
            Thou slave, thou wretch, thou coward,
Thou little valiant, great in villainy!
Thou ever strong upon the stronger side!
Thou fortune's champion, that dost never fight
But when her humorous ladyship is by
To teach thee safety!

        .   .   .   .   .   .

Thou wear a lion's hide! Doff it for shame,
And hang a calf's skin on those recreant limbs.
                                      Act iii. Sc. 1.
Life is as tedious as a twicetold tale,
Vexing the dull ear of a drowsy man.   Act iii. Sc. 4.
To gild refined gold, to paint the lily,
To throw a perfume on the violet,

To smooth the ice, or add another hue
Unto the rainbow, or with taper-light
To seek the beauteous eye of heaven to garnish,
Is wasteful and ridiculous excess.   *Act iv. Sc. 2.*
How oft the sight of means to do ill deeds
Makes deeds ill done!   *Act iv. Sc. 2.*

KING RICHARD II.

Oh, who can hold a fire in his hand,
By thinking on the frosty Caucasus?
Or cloy the hungry edge of appetite,
By bare imagination of a feast?
    The apprehension of the good
Gives but the greater feeling to the worse.

     Act i. Sc. 3.
The ripest fruit first falls.   *Act ii. Sc. 1.*

FIRST PART OF KING HENRY IV.

'T is my vocation, Hal; 't is no sin for a man to labor
in his vocation.   *Act i. Sc. 2.*
He will give the Devil his due.   *Act i. Sc. 2.*
And, as the soldiers bore dead bodies by,
He called them untaught knaves, unmannerly,
To bring a slovenly, unhandsome corse
Betwixt the wind and his nobility.   *Act i. Sc. 3.*
By heaven, methinks it were an easy leap,
To pluck bright honor from the pale-faced moon.

     Act i. Sc. 3.
I know a trick worth two of that.   *Act ii. Sc. 1.*
Call you that backing of your friends? a plague upon
such backing!   *Act ii. Sc. 4.*
A plague of sighing and grief! it blows a man up like a
bladder.   *Act ii. Sc. 4.*
Give you a reason on compulsion! if reasons were as
plenty as blackberries, I would give no man a reason upon
compulsion.   *Act ii. Sc. 4.*
I was a coward on instinct.   *Act ii. Sc. 4.*
No more of that, Hal, an thou lovest me.   *Act ii. Sc. 4.*
Glen. I can call spirits from the vasty deep,
Hot. Why, so can I, or so can any man:
But will they come when you do call for them?

     Act iii. Sc. 1.

Tell truth and shame the Devil.   Act iii. Sc. 1.
I had rather be a kitten, and cry mew,
Than one of these same metre ballad-mongers.
    Act iii. Sc. 1.
Shall I not take mine ease in mine inn?   Act iii. Sc. 3.
I could have better spared a better man.   Act v. Sc. 4.
The better part of valor is — discretion.   Act v. Sc. 4.
Lord, Lord, how this world is given to lying! I grant
you, I was down, and out of breath; and so was he: but
we rose both at an instant, and fought a long hour by
Shrewsbury clock.   Act v. Sc. 4.

SECOND PART OF KING HENRY IV.

Even such a man, so faint, so spiritless,
So dull, so dead in look, so woe-begone,
Drew Priam's curtain in the dead of night,
And would have told him, half his Troy was burned.
    Act i. Sc. 1.
Yet the first bringer of unwelcome news
Hath but a losing office; and his tongue
Sounds ever after as a sullen bell,
Remembered knolling a departed friend.
    Act i. Sc. 1.
I am not only witty in myself, but the cause that wit
is in other men.   Act i. Sc. 2.
He hath eaten me out of house and home.   Act ii. Sc. 2.
    He was, indeed, the glass
Wherein the noble youth did dress themselves.
    Act ii. Sc. 3.
    Sleep, gentle sleep,
Nature's soft nurse, how have I frighted thee,
That thou no more wilt weigh my eyelids down,
And steep my senses in forgetfulness?
    Act iii. Sc. 1.
With all appliances and means to boot.   Act iii. Sc. 1.
Uneasy lies the head that wears a crown.   Act iii. Sc. 1.
He hath a tear for pity, and a hand
Open as day for melting charity.   Act iv. Sc. 4.
Thy wish was father, Harry, to that thought.
    Act iv. Sc. 4.
Under which king, Bezonian? Speak, or die.
    Act v. Sc. 3.

KING HENRY V.

Consideration like an angel came,
And whipped the offending Adam out of him.
Act i. Sc. 1.

When he speaks,
The air, a chartered libertine, is still.   Act i. Sc. 1.
Base is the slave that pays.   Act ii. Sc. 1.
'A babbled of green fields.   Act ii. Sc. 3.
With busy hammers closing rivets up,
Give dreadful note of preparation.   Act iv. Chorus.

Then shall our names,
Familiar in their mouths as household words, —
Harry the King, Bedford and Exeter,
Warwick and Talbot, Salisbury and Gloster, —
Be in their flowing cups freshly remembered.
Act iv. Sc. 3.

FIRST PART OF KING HENRY VI.

She 's beautiful: and therefore to be wooed:
She is a woman; therefore to be won.   Act v. Sc. 3.

SECOND PART OF KING HENRY VI.

Smooth runs the water where the brook is deep.
Act iii. Sc. 1.
What stronger breastplate than a heart untainted?
Thrice is he armed that hath his quarrel just;
And he but naked, though locked up in steel,
Whose conscience with injustice is corrupted.
Act iii. Sc. 2.
He dies and makes no sign.   Act iii. Sc. 3.

THIRD PART OF KING HENRY VI.

Suspicion always haunts the guilty mind;
The thief doth fear each bush an officer.   Act v. Sc. 6.

KING RICHARD III.

Now is the winter of our discontent
Made glorious summer by this sun of York;

And all the clouds that lowered upon our house,
In the deep bosom of the ocean buried.   Act i. Sc. 1.
Cheated of feature by dissembling nature,
Deformed, unfinished, sent before my time
Into this breathing world, scarce half made up.
                                         Act i. Sc. 1.
Why I, in this weak, piping time of peace,
Have no delight to pass away the time.   Act i. Sc. 1.
To leave this keen encounter of our wits.   Act i. Sc. 2.
Was ever woman in this humor wooed?
Was ever woman in this humor won?   Act i. Sc. 2.
O, I have passed a miserable night,
So full of fearful dreams, of ugly sights,
That, as I am a Christian faithful man,
I would not spend another such a night,
Though 't were to buy a world of happy days.
                                         Act i. Sc. 4.
Thou troublest me; I am not in the vein.   Act iv. Sc. 2.
Let not the heavens hear these telltale women
Rail on the Lord's anointed.   Act iv. Sc. 4.
An honest tale speeds best, being plainly told.
                                         Act iv. Sc. 4.
Thus far into the bowels of the land
Have we marched on without impediment.   Act v. Sc. 2.
True hope is swift, and flies with swallow's wings,
Kings it makes gods, and meaner creatures kings.
                                         Act v. Sc. 2.
The king's name is a tower of strength.   Act v. Sc. 3.
       I have set my life upon a cast,
And I will stand the hazard of the die.   Act v. Sc. 4.
A horse! a horse! My kingdom for a horse!   Act v. Sc. 4.

KING HENRY VIII.

Verily

I swear, 't is better to be lowly born,
And range with humble livers in content,
Than to be perked up in a glistering grief,
And wear a golden sorrow.   Act ii. Sc. 3.
       And then to breakfast with
What appetite you have.   Act iii. Sc. 2.
Farewell, a long farewell, to all my greatness!

This is the state of man. To-day he puts forth
The tender leaves of hope, to-morrow blossoms,
And bears his blushing honors thick upon him.
Act iii. Sc. 2.

O how wretched

Is that poor man that hangs on princes' favors!
There is, betwixt that smile we would aspire to,
That sweet aspect of princes, and their ruin,
More pangs and fears than wars or women have;
And when he falls, he falls like Lucifer,
Never to hope again.   Act iii. Sc. 2.
Had I but served my God with half the zeal
I served my king, he would not in mine age
Have left me naked to mine enemies.
Act iii. Sc. 2.

Men's evil manners live in brass; their virtues
We write in water.   Act iv. Sc. 2.
To dance attendance on their lordships' pleasures.
Act v. Sc. 2.

TROILUS AND CRESSIDA

One touch of nature makes the whole world kin.
Act iii. Sc. 3.

And, like a dew-drop from the lion's mane,
Be shook to air.   Act iii. Sc. 3.

CORIOLANUS

Hear you this Triton of the minnows?   Act iii. Sc. 1.

JULIUS CAESAR

Beware the Ides of March!   Act i. Sc. 2.
I cannot tell what you and other men
Think of this life! but for my single self,
I had as lief not be, as live to be
In awe of such a thing as I myself.   Act i. Sc. 2.

Dar'st thou, Cassius, now

Leap in with me into this angry flood,
And swim to yonder point? — Upon the word,
Accoutred as I was, I plunged in,
And bade him follow.   Act i. Sc. 2.

Ye gods, it doth amaze me,

A man of such a feeble temper should

So get the start of the majestic world,
And bear the palm alone.   Act i. Sc. 2
Why, man, he doth bestride the narrow world,
Like a Colossus, and we petty men
Walk under his huge legs, and peep about
To find ourselves dishonorable graves.   Act i. Sc. 2.
Let me have men about me, that are fat;
Sleek-headed men, and such as sleep o' nights;
Yond' Cassius has a lean and hungry look;
He thinks too much: such men are dangerous.
                                            Act i. Sc. 2.
Seldom he smiles; and smiles in such a sort,
As if he mocked himself, and scorned his spirit,
That could be moved to smile at anything.   Act i. Sc. 2.
But, for mine own part, it was Greek to me. Act i. Sc. 2.
Between the acting of a dreadful thing
And the first motion, all the interim is
Like phantasma, or a hideous dream.
                                            Act ii. Sc. 1.
You are my true and honorable wife,
As dear to me as the ruddy drops
That visit my sad heart.   Act ii. Sc. 1.
Cowards die many times before their deaths;
The valiant never taste of death but once.
                                            Act ii. Sc. 2.
Though last, not least, in love.   Act iii. Sc. 1.
Cry *Havoc*, and let slip the dogs of war. Act iii. Sc. 1.
Romans, countrymen, and lovers! hear me for my cause;
and be silent that you may hear.   Act iii. Sc. 2.
Not that I loved Caesar less, but that I loved Rome more.
                                            Act iii. Sc. 2.
Who is here so base, that would be a bondman? If any,
speak: for him have I offended.   Act iii. Sc. 2.
The evil that men do lives after them;
The good is oft interred with their bones.
                                            Act iii. Sc. 2.
For Brutus is an honorable man;
So are they all, all honorable men.   Act iii. Sc. 2.
When that the poor have cried, Caesar hath wept;
Ambition should be made of sterner stuff.   Act iii. Sc. 2.
But yesterday, the word of Caesar might
Have stood against the world; now lies he there,

And none so poor to do him reverence.

Act iii. Sc. 2.

If you have tears, prepare to shed them now.

Act iii. Sc. 2.

See, what a rent the envious Casca made!   Act iii. Sc. 2.

This was the most unkindest cut of all.   Act iii. Sc. 2.

Great Caesar fell.

O what a fall was there, my countrymen!

Act iii. Sc. 2.

Put a tongue

In every wound of Caesar, that should move
The stones of Rome to rise and mutiny.   Act iii. Sc. 2.

There are no tricks in plain and simple faith.

Act iv. Sc. 2.

I had rather be a dog, and bay the moon,
Than such a Roman.   Act iv. Sc. 3.

There is no terror, Cassius, in your threats;
For I am armed so strong in honesty,
That they pass by me as the idle wind,
Which I respect not.   Act iv. Sc. 3.

A friend should bear a friend's infirmities,
But Brutus makes mine greater than they are.

Act iv. Sc. 3.

There is a tide in the affairs of men,
Which, taken at the flood, leads on to fortune;
Omitted, all the voyage of their life
Is bound in shallows, and in miseries.

Act iv. Sc. 3.

His life was gentle, and the elements
So mixed in him, that nature might stand up
And say to all the world, *This was a man!*   Act v. Sc. 5.

ANTONY AND CLEOPATRA

There's beggary in the love that can be reckoned.

Act i. Sc. 1.

For her own person,

It beggared all description.   Act ii. Sc. 2.

Age cannot wither her, nor custom stale
Her infinite variety.   Act ii. Sc. 2.

CYMBELINE

Hark! hark! the lark at heaven's gate sings.

Act ii. Sc. 3.

Some griefs are med'cinable.   Act iii. Sc. 2.

Weariness

Can snore upon the flint, when restive sloth
Finds the down pillow hard.   Act iii. Sc. 6.

KING LEAR

How sharper than a serpent's tooth it is,
To have a thankless child.   Act i. Sc. 4.
Striving to better, oft we mar what's well.   Act i. Sc. 4.
O, let not women's weapons, water-drops,
Stain my man's cheeks.   Act ii. Sc. 4.
Blow, wind, and crack your cheeks! rage! blow!
Act iii. Sc. 2.

Tremble, thou wretch,

That hast within thee undivulged crimes,
Unwhipped of justice.   Act iii. Sc. 2.

I am a man

More sinned against than sinning.   Act iii. Sc. 2.

Poor naked wretches, wheresoe'er you are,
That bide the pelting of this pitiless storm,
How shall your houseless heads, and unfed sides,
Your looped and windowed raggedness, defend you
From seasons such as these?

.   .   .   .

Take physic, pomp;

Expose thyself to feel what wretches feel.   Act iii. Sc. 4.
I'll talk a word with this same learned Theban.
Act iii. Sc. 4.

The little dogs and all,

Tray, Blanch, and Sweet-heart, see, they bark at me.
Act iii. Sc. 6.
Ay, every inch a king.   Act iv. Sc. 6.
Give me an ounce of civet, good apothecary, to sweet-
en my imagination.   Act iv. Sc. 6.
Through tattered clothes small vices do appear;
Robes and furred gowns hide all.   Act iv. Sc. 6.
The gods are just, and of our pleasant vices
Make instruments to scourge us.   Act v. Sc. 3.

Her voice was ever soft,

Gentle, and low; an excellent thing in woman.
Act v. Sc. 3.

ROMEO AND JULIET

The weakest goes to the wall.	Act i. Sc. 1.

One fire burns out another burning.
One pain is lessened by another's anguish. Act i. Sc. 2.
Too early seen unknown, and known too late.
                                                        Act i. Sc. 5.
He jests at scars, that never felt a wound. Act ii. Sc. 2.
See, how she leans her cheek upon her hand!
O that I were a glove upon that hand,
That I might touch that cheek!   Act ii. Sc. 2.
O Romeo, Romeo! wherefore art thou Romeo?
                                                        Act ii. Sc. 2.
What's in a name? that which we call a rose
By any other name would smell as sweet.
                                                        Act ii. Sc. 2.
Alack! there lies more peril in thine eye,
Than twenty of their swords.   Act ii. Sc. 2.
                At lover's perjuries,
They say, Jove laughs.   Act ii. Sc. 2.
O swear not by the moon, the inconstant moon,
That monthly changes in her circled orb,
Lest that thy love prove likewise variable. Act ii. Sc. 2.
Good night, good night! parting is such sweet sorrow,
That I shall say good night till it be morrow.
                                                        Act ii. Sc. 2.
Thy old groans ring yet in my ancient ears. Act ii. Sc. 3.
Stabbed with a white wench's black eye.
                                                        Act ii. Sc. 4.
I am the very pink of courtesy.   Act ii. Sc. 4.
My man's as true as steel.   Act ii. Sc. 4.
Here comes the lady; — O, so light a foot
Will ne'ver wear out the everlasting flint. Act ii. Sc. 6.
A plague o' both the houses!   Act iii. Sc. 1.
Rom. Courage, man! the hurt cannot be much.
Mer. No, 't not so deep as a well, nor so wide as
a church-door; but 't is enough.   Act iii. Sc. 1.
Adversity's sweet milk, philosophy.   Act iii. Sc. 3.
Night's candles are burnt out, and jocund day
Stands tiptoe on the misty mountain-tops. Act ii. Sc. 5.
Not stepping o'er the bounds of modesty. Act iv. Sc. 2.
My bosom's lord sits lightly in his throne. Act v. Sc. 1.
A beggarly account of empty boxes.   Act v. Sc. 1.

My poverty, but not my will, consents.   Act v. Sc. 1.
                    Beauty's ensign yet
Is crimson in thy lips, and in thy cheeks,
And death's pale flag is not advanced there.
                                          Act v. Sc. 3.

                    Eyes, look your last!
Arms, take your last embrace!

HAMLET

This bodes some strange eruption to our state.
                                          Act i. Sc. 1.
In the most high and palmy state of Rome,
A little ere the mightiest Julius fell,
The graves stood tenantless, and the sheeted dead
Did squeak and gibber in the Roman streets.
                                          Act i. Sc. 1.

And then it started like a guilty thing
Upon a fearful summons.   Act i. Sc. 1.
Some say, that ever 'gainst that season comes
Wherein our Saviour's birth is celebrated,
This bird of dawning singeth all night long:
And then they say no spirit dares stir abroad,
The nights are wholesome; then no planets strike,
No fairy takes, nor witch hath power to charm,
So hallowed and so gracious is the time.   Act i. Sc. 1.
The head is not more native to the heart.   Act i. Sc. 2.
A little more than kin, and less than kind. Act i. Sc. 2.
Seems, madam! nay, it is; I know not seems.
                                          Act i. Sc. 2.

But I have that within which passeth show;
These, but the trappings and the suits of woe.
                                          Act i. Sc. 2.

O that this too, too solid flesh would melt,
Thaw, and resolve itself into a dew!
Or that the Everlasting had not fixed
His canon 'gainst self-slaughter! O God! O God!
How weary, stale, flat, and unprofitable
Seem to me all the uses of this world! . . .
                    That it should come to this! . . .
Hyperion to a satyr! so loving to my mother,
That he might not beteem the winds of heaven

Visit her face too roughly. . . .
Why, she would hang on him,
As if increase of appetite had grown
By what it fed on. . . .
Frailty, thy name is woman!
A little month.
Like Niobe, all tears.
My father's brother; but no more like my father
Than I to Hercules.

Act i. Sc. 2.

Thrift, thrift, Horatio! the funeral baked meats
Did coldly furnish forth the marriage tables.

Act i. Sc. 2.

In my mind's eye, Horatio.   Act i. Sc. 2.
He was a man, take him for all in all,
I shall not look upon his like again.   Act i. Sc. 2.
A countenance more
In sorrow than in anger.   Act i. Sc. 2.
And in the morn and liquid dew of youth.   Act i. Sc. 3.
Be thou familiar, but by no means vulgar.
The friends thou hast, and their adoption tried,
Grapple them to thy soul with hooks of steel. . . .
Give every man thy ear, but few thy voice.
Costly thy habit as thy purse can buy,
But not expressed in fancy; rich, not gaudy;
For the apparel oft proclaims the man.
Neither a borrower nor a lender be.
Springes to catch woodcocks.   Act i. Sc. 3.
But to my mind, — though I am native here,
And to the manner born, — it is a custom
More honored in the breach than the observance.

Act i. Sc. 4.

Angels and ministers of grace, defend us!   Act i. Sc. 4.
Thou com'st in such a questionable shape,
That I will speak to thee.   Act i. Sc. 4.
Let me not burst in ignorance!   Act i. Sc. 4.
I do not set my life at a pin's fee.   Act i. Sc. 4.
Something is rotten in the state of Denmark.

Act i. Sc. 4.

I could a tale unfold, whose lightest word
Would harrow up thy soul; freeze thy young blood;
Make thy two eyes, like stars, start from their spheres;

Thy knotted and combined locks to part,
And each particular hair to stand on end,
Like quills upon the fretful Porcupine.   Act i. Sc. 5.
O my prophetic soul! my uncle!   Act i. Sc. 5.
O Hamlet, what a falling-off was there!   Act i. Sc. 5.
No reckoning made, but sent to my account
With all my imperfections on my head.   Act i. Sc. 5.
The glow-worm shows the matin to be near,
And 'gins to pale his uneffectual fire.   Act i. Sc. 5.
There needs no ghost, my lord, come from the grave,
To tell us this.   Act i. Sc. 5.
There are more things in heaven and earth, Horatio,
Than are dreamt of in your philosophy.   Act i. Sc. 5.
The time is out of joint.   Act i. Sc. 5.
This is the very ecstasy of love.   Act ii. Sc. 1.
    Brevity is the soul of wit.   Act ii. Sc. 2.
That he is mad, 't is true; 't is true, 't is pity;
And pity 't is, 't is true.   Act ii. Sc. 2.
       Doubt thou the stars are fire;
       Doubt that the sun doth move;
       Doubt truth to be a liar;
       But never doubt I love.
    Act ii. Sc. 2.
Still harping on my daughter.   Act ii. Sc. 2.
Though this be madness, yet there 's method in it.
    Act ii. Sc. 2.
What a piece of work is man! How noble in reason!
how infinite in faculties! in form and moving, how express
and admirable! in action, how like an angel! in apprehen-
sion, how like a God!   Act ii. Sc. 2.
Man delights not me, — nor woman neither.
    Act ii. Sc. 2.
I know a hawk from a hand-saw.   Act ii. Sc. 2.
Come, give us a taste of your quality.   Act ii. Sc. 2.
'T was caviare to the general.   Act ii. Sc. 2.
What 's Hecuba to him, or he to Hecuba?
    Act ii. Sc. 2.
       The play 's the thing,
Wherein I'll catch the conscience of the king.
    Act ii. Sc. 2.
To be, or not to be? that is the question: —
Whether 't is nobler in the mind, to suffer

The slings and arrows of outrageous fortune,
Or to take arms against a sea of troubles,
And, by opposing, end them? — To die — to sleep —
No more; — and, by a sleep, to say we end
The heart-ache, and the thousand natural shocks
That flesh is heir to; — 't is a consummation
Devoutly to be wished. To die; — to sleep; —
To sleep! perchance, to dream: — ay, there 's the rub;
For in that sleep of death what dreams may come,
When we have shuffled off this mortal coil,
Must give us pause. . . .
                                    The spurns
That patient merit of the unworthy takes;
When he himself might his quietus make
With a bare bodkin. Who would fardels bear,
To grunt and sweat under a weary life,
But that the dread of something after death —
The undiscovered country, from whose bourne
No traveller returns — puzzles the will,
And makes us rather bear those ills we have,
Than fly to others that we know not of?
Thus conscience does make cowards of us all,
And thus the native hue of resolution
Is sicklied o'er with the pale cast of thought. . . .
                    Nymph, in thy orisons
Be all my sins remembered.
                                    Act iii. Sc. 1.
    Be thou as chaste as ice, as pure as snow, thou shalt
not escape calumny.   Act iii. Sc. 1.
The glass of fashion, and the mould of form,
The observed of all observers!   Act iii. Sc. 1.
Now see that noble and most sovereign reason,
Like sweet bells jangled, out of tune and harsh.
                                    Act iii. Sc. 1.
    It out-herods Herod.   Act iii. Sc. 2.
    Suit the action to the word, the word to the action.
                                    Act iii. Sc. 2.
    To hold, as 't were, the mirror up to nature.
                                    Act iii. Sc. 2.
    I have thought some of nature's journeymen had made
men, and not made them well, they imitated humanity so
abominably.   Act iii. Sc. 2.

No, let the candied tongue lick absurd pomp;
And crook the pregnant hinges of the knee,
Where thrift may follow fawning.   Act iii. Sc. 2.
    Give me that man
That is not passion 's slave, and I will wear him
In my heart's core, ay, in my heart of hearts,
As I do thee.   Act iii. Sc. 2.
Something too much of this.   Act iii. Sc. 2.
Here 's metal more attractive.   Act iii. Sc. 2.
 The lady doth protest too much, methinks.

         Act iii. Sc. 2.
 Let the galled jade wince, our withers are unwrung.
         Act iii. Sc. 2.

  Why, let the strucken deer go weep,
   The hart ungalled play;
  For some must watch, while some must sleep;
   Thus runs the world away.   Act iii. Sc. 2.
It will discourse most eloquent music.   Act iii. Sc. 2.
Very like a whale.   Act iii. Sc. 2.
They fool me to the top of my bent.   Act iii. Sc. 2.
'T is now the very witching time of night,
When churchyards yawn, and hell itself breathes out
Contagion to this world.   Act iii. Sc. 2.
O my offence is rank, it smells to heaven.   Act iii. Sc. 3.
Look here, upon this picture, and on this;
The counterfeit presentment of two brothers.
         Act iii. Sc. 4.

See what a grace was seated on this brow!
Hyperion's curls; the front of Jove himself;
An eye like Mars, to threaten and command. . . .
A combination, and a form, indeed,
Where every god did seem to set his seal,
To give the world assurance of a man.   Act iii. Sc. 4.
A king of shreds and patches.   Act iii. Sc. 4.
This is the very coinage of your brain.   Act iii. Sc. 4.
Lay not that flattering unction to your soul.   Act iii. Sc. 4.
Assume a virtue, if you have it not.   Act iii. Sc. 4.
For 't is the sport, to have the engineer
Hoist with his own petar.   Act iii. Sc. 4.
When horrors come, they come not single spies,
But in battalions!   Act iv. Sc. 5.
There 's such divinity doth hedge a king,

That treason can but peep to what it would.

Act iv. Sc. 5.

How absolute the knave is! we must speak by the card, or equivocation will undo us.   Act v. Sc. 1.

Alas, poor Yorick; I knew him, Horatio: a fellow of infinite jest; of most excellent fancy.   Act v. Sc. 1.

Where be your gibes now? your gambols? your songs? your flashes of merriment, that were wont to set the table on a roar?   Act v. Sc. 1.

To what base uses we may return, Horatio!

Act v. Sc. 1.

Imperial Caesar, dead, and turned to clay,
Might stop a hole to keep the wind away.   Act v. Sc. 1.
Sir, though I am not splenetive and rash,
Yet have I in me something dangerous.   Act v. Sc. 1.
The cat will mew, and dog will have his day.

Act v. Sc. 1.

There's a divinity that shapes our ends,
Rough-hew them how we will.   Act v. Sc. 2.
There is a special providence in the fall of a sparrow.

Act v. Sc. 2.

A hit, a very palpable hit.   Act v. Sc. 2.

OTHELLO

But I will wear my heart upon my sleeve
For daws to peck at.   Act i. Sc. 1.
Most potent, grave, and reverend seigniors.   Act i. Sc. 3.
The very head and front of my offending
Hath this extent, no more.   Act i. Sc. 3.
I will a round, unvarnished tale deliver
Of my whole course of love.   Act i. Sc. 3.
Wherein I spoke of most disastrous chances,
Of moving accidents, by flood and field;
Of hair-breadth 'scapes i' the imminent deadly breach.

Act i. Sc. 3.

My story being done,
She gave me for my pains a world of sighs:
She swore, In faith, 't was strange, 't was passing strange;
'T was pitiful, 't was wondrous pitiful:
She wished she had not heard it; yet she wished
That Heaven had made her such a man.

Act i. Sc. 3.

Upon this hint I spoke.   Act i. Sc. 3.
I do perceive here a divided duty.   Act i. Sc. 3.
For I am nothing, if not critical.   Act ii. Sc. 1.
Iago. To suckle fools, and chronicle small beer.
Des. O most lame and impotent conclusion!
                                           Act ii. Sc. 1.
Silence that dreadful bell; it frights the isle
From her propriety.   Act ii. Sc. 3.
    O thou invisible spirit of wine, if thou hast no name
to be known by, let us call thee devil!   Act ii. Sc. 3.
    O that men should put an enemy in their mouths, to
steal away their brains!   Act ii. Sc. 3.
                    Perdition catch my soul,
But I do love thee! and when I love thee not,
Chaos is come again.   Act iii. Sc. 3.
Good name, in man and woman, dear my lord,
Is the immediate jewel of their souls.
Who steals my purse, steals trash; 't is something nothing;
'T was mine, 't is his, and has been slave to thousands;
But he that filches from me my good name
Robs me of that which not enriches him,
And makes me poor indeed.   Act ii. Sc. 3.
                    O, beware, my lord, of jealousy;
It is the green-eyed monster, which doth make
The meat it feeds on.   Act iii. Sc. 3.
                    Trifles, light as air,
Are, to the jealous, confirmations strong
As proofs of holy writ.   Act iii. Sc. 3.
                    Not poppy, nor mandragora,
Nor all the drowsy sirups of the world,
Shall ever medicine thee to that sweet sleep
Which thou ow'dst yesterday.   Act iii. Sc. 3.
He that is robbed, not wanting what is stolen,
Let him not know it, and he's not robbed at all.
                                           Act iii. Sc. 3.
                O, now, for ever,
Farewell the tranquil mind! farewell content!
Farewell the plumed troop, and the big wars,
That make ambition virtue! O farewell!
Farewell the neighing steed, and the shrill trump,
The spirit-stirring drum, the ear-piercing fife,

.   .   .   .   .   .

Othello's occupation 's gone!

Act iii. Sc. 3.

Give me the ocular proof. Act iii. Sc. 3.

But this denoted a foregone conclusion. Act iii. Sc. 3.

They laugh that win. Act iv. Sc. 1.

Steeped me in poverty to the very lips. Act iv. Sc. 2.

But, alas! to make me
A fixed figure, for the time of scorn
To point his slow, unmoving finger at.

Act iv. Sc. 2.

And put in every honest hand a whip,
To lash the rascal naked through the world.

Act iv. Sc. 2.

'T is neither here nor there. Act iv. Sc. 3.

He hath a daily beauty in his life. Act v. Sc. 1.

I have done the state some service, and they know it.

Act v. Sc. 2.

Speak of me as I am; nothing extenuate,
Nor set down aught in malice. Then must you speak
Of one that loved not wisely, but too well. . . .
Of one, whose hand,
Like the base Judean, threw a pearl away,
Richer than all his tribe. . . .
Albeit unused to the melting mood.

THOMAS TUSSER — (1523-1580)

Except wind stands as never it stood,
It is an ill wind turns none to good.
Moral Reflections on the Wind.

FULKE GREVILLE, LORD BROOKE — (1554-1624)

O wearisome condition of humanity!
Mustapha. Act v. Sc. 4.

And out of minde as soon as out of sight. *Sonnet LVI.*

CHRISTOPHER MARLOWE — (1565-1593)

Who ever loved that loved not at first sight?
Hero and Leander.

Come live with me, and be my love,
And we will all the pleasures prove
That valleys, groves, and hills, and folds,

Woods, or steepy mountains, yield.

The Passionate Shepherd to his Love.

SIR WALTER RALEIGH — (1552-1618)

If all the world and love were young,
And truth in every shepherd's tongue,
These pretty pleasures might me move
To live with thee, and be thy love.

The Nymph's Reply to the Passionate Shepherd.

Silence in love bewrays more love
    Than words, though ne'er so witty;
A beggar that is dumb, you know,
    May challenge double pity.

The Silent Lover.

JOSHUA SYLVESTER — (1563-1618)

Go, Soul, the body's guest,
    Upon a thankless errand!
Fear not to touch the best:
    The truth shall be thy warrant.
Go, since I needs must die,
And give the world the lie.

*The Soul's Errand.**

RICHARD BARNFIELD

As it fell upon a day,
In the merry month of May,
Sitting in a pleasant shade
Which a grove of myrtles made.

*Address to the Nightingale.***

EDMUND SPENSER — (1553-1597)

FAERIE QUEENE

The noblest mind the best contentment has.

Book i. Canto i. St. 35.

---

* Sylvester is now generally regarded as the author of "The Soul's Errand," long attributed to Raleigh.

** This song, often attributed to Shakespeare, is now confidently assigned to Barnfield, and it is found in his collection of Poems, published between 1594 and 1598.

Her angels face,

As the great eye of heaven, shyned bright,
And made a sunshine in the shady place.

Book 1. Canto iii. St. 4.

That darkesome cave they enter, where they find
That cursed man, low sitting on the ground,
Musing full sadly in his sullein mind.

Book i. Canto ix. St. 35.

No daintie flowre or herbe that growes on grownd
No arborett with painted blossomes drest
And smelling sweete, but there it might be fownd
To bud out faire, and throwe her sweete smels al arownd.

Book ii. Canto vi. St. 12.

Dan Chaucer, well of English undefyled.

Book iv. Canto ii. St. 32.

I was promised on a time
To have reason for my rhyme;
From that time unto this season,
I received nor rhyme nor reason.

Lines on his Promised Pension.

For of the soul the body form doth take
For soul is form, and doth the Body make.

Hymn in Honor of Beauty. Line 132.

MOTHER HUBBERDS TALE

Full little knowest thou that hast not tride,
What hell it is in suing long to bide;
To loose good dayes, that might be better spent;
To wast long nights in pensive discontent;
To speed to-day, to be put back to-morrow;
To feed on hope, to pine with fear and sorrow; . . .
To fret thy soule with crosses and with cares;
To eate thy heart through comfortlesse dispaires;
To fawne, to crowche, to waite, to ride, to ronne,
To spend, to give, to want, to be undonne.

SIR HENRY WOTTON — (1568-1639)

How happy is he born and taught,
That serveth not another's will;
Whose armor is his honest thought,
And simple truth his utmost skill!

•   •   •   •

Lord of himself, though not of lands;
And having nothing, yet hath all.
The Character of a Happy Life.
You meaner beauties of the night,
That poorly satisfy our eyes
More by your number than your light!
To his Mistress, the Queen of Bohemia.

DR. JOHN DONNE — (1573-1631)

Funeral elegies, on the progress of the soul

We understood
Her by her sight; her pure and eloquent blood
Spoke in her cheeks, and so distinctly wrought,
That one might almost say her body thought.
The Second Anniversary. Line 245.
She and comparisons are odious.
Elegy 8. The Comparison.

BEN JONSON — (1574-1637)

To Celia

[From "The Forest."]
Drink to me only with thine eyes,
And I will pledge with mine;
Or leave a kiss but in the cup,
And I'll not look for wine.

The Sweet Neglect

[From the "Silent Woman." Act i. Sc. 5.]

Still to be neat, still to be drest
As you were going to a feast.
Give me a look, give me a face,
That makes simplicity a grace.

Good Life, Long Life

In small proportion we just beauties see,
And in short measures life may perfect be.

Epitaph on Elizabeth

Underneath this stone doth lie

As much beauty as could die;
Which in life did harbor give
To more virtue than doth live.

Epitaph on the Countess of Pembroke

Underneath this sable hearse
Lies the subject of all verse,
Sidney's sister, Pembroke's mother.
Death! ere thou hast slain another,
Learned and fair and good as she,
Time shall throw a dart at thee.

To the Memory of Shakespeare

Soul of the age!
The applause! delight! the wonder of our stage!
My Shakespeare rise.

.   .   .   .   .

Small Latin, and less Greek.

.   .   .   .   .   .

He was not of an age, but for all time.

.   .   .   .   .

Sweet swan of Avon!

Every Man in his Humor. Act ii. Sc. 3.

Get money; still get money, boy;
No matter by what means.

FRANCIS BEAUMONT — (1585-1616)

Letter to Ben Jonson

What things have we seen
Done at the Mermaid! heard words that have been
So nimble, and so full of subtile flame,
As if that every one from whence they came
Had meant to put his whole wit in a jest,
And resolved to live a fool the rest
Of his dull life.

GEORGE WITHER — (1588-1667)

The Shepherd's Resolution

Shall I, wasting in despair,

Die because a woman's fair?
Or make pale my cheeks with care,
'Cause another's rosie are?
    If she be not so to me,
    What care I how fair she be?

FRANCIS QUARLES — (1592-1644)

Be wisely worldly, be not worldly wise.

Emblems. Book ii. 2

This house is to be let for life or years;
Her rent is sorrow, and her income tears;
Cupid 't has long stood void; her bills make known,
She must be dearly let, or let alone.

Book ii. Epigram 10.

GEORGE HERBERT — (1593-1632)

Virtue

Sweet day, so cool, so calm, so bright,
The bridall of the earth and skies.

Only a sweet and virtuous soul,
Like seasoned timber, never gives.

SIR JOHN SUCKLING — (1608-1644)

On a Wedding

Her feet beneath her petticoat,
Like little mice, stole in and out,
    As if they feared the light;
But oh! she dances such a way!
No sun upon an Easter-day
    Is half so fine a sight.
Her lips were red, and one was thin,
Compared with that was next her chin,
    Some bee had stung it newly.

Song

Why so pale and wan, fond lover,

Prithee, why so pale?
Will, when looking well can 't move her,
Looking ill prevail?
Prithee, why so pale?

ROBERT HERRICK — (1591-1660)

The Rock of Rubies, and the Quarrie of Pearls

Some asked me where the Rubies grew,
And nothing I did say;
But with my finger pointed to
The lips of Julia.
Some asked how Pearls did grow, and where?
Then spoke I to my Girl,
To part her lips, and showed them there
The quarelets of Pearl.

On her Feet

Her pretty feet, like snails, did creep
A little out, and then,
As if they played at Bo-peep,
Did soon draw in again.

To the Virgins to make much of Time

Gather ye rosebuds while ye may,
Old Time is still a-flying,
And this same flower, that smiles to-day,
To-morrow will be dying.

Night Piece to Julia

Her eyes the glow-worm lend thee,
The shooting stars attend thee;
And the elves also,
Whose little eyes glow
Like the sparks of fire, befriend thee.

SIR RICHARD LOVELACE — (1618-1658)

Orpheus to Beasts

Oh! could you view the melody

Of every grace,
And music of her face,
You'd drop a tear;
Seeing more harmony
In her bright eye,
Than now you hear.

To Lucasta on going to the Wars

I could not love thee, dear, so much,
Loved I not honor more.

To Althea from Prison

Stone walls do not a prison make,
Nor iron barres a cage;
Mindes innocent, and quiet, take
That for an hermitage.

JAMES SHIRLEY — (1596-1666)

Contention of Ajax and Ulysses. Sc. iii.

Death's Final Conquest

Only the actions of the just
Smell sweet and blossom in the dust.

RICHARD CRASHAW — (-1650)

The conscious water saw its God and blushed.*

In Praise of Lessius' Rule of Health

A happy soul, that all the way
To heaven hath a summer's day.

THOMAS DEKKER — (-1638)

Old Fortunatus

And though mine arm should conquer twenty worlds,
There's lean fellow beats all conquerors.

---

* Lympha pudica Deum vidit et erubuit. — *Latin Poems.*

Honest Whore. P. ii. Act i. Sc. 2.

We are ne'er like angels till our passion dies.

ABRAHAM COWLEY — (1618-1667)

The Waiting-Maid

Th' adorning thee with so much art
    Is but a barb'rous skill;
'T is like the poisoning of a dart,
    Too apt before to kill.

The Motto

What shall I do to be for ever known,
And make the age to come my own?

On the Death of Crashaw

His *faith,* perhaps, in some nice tenets might
Be wrong; his *life,* I'm sure, was in the right.

The Garden. Essay V.

God the first garden made, and the first city Cain.

SIR JOHN DENHAM — (1615-1668)

Cooper's Hill. Line 189.

O could I flow like thee, and make thy stream
My great example, as it is my theme!
Though deep, yet clear; though gentle, yet not dull;
Strong without rage; without o'erflowing, full.

The Sophy. A Tragedy

Actions of the last age are like Almanacs of the last year.

THOMAS CAREW — (1589-1639)

Disdain Returned

He that loves a rosy cheek,
    Or a coral lip admires,
    Or from star-like eyes doth seek

Fuel to maintain his fires;
As old Time makes these decay,
So his flames must waste away.

Conquest by Flight

Then fly betimes, for only they
Conquer love, that run away.

EDMUND WALLER — (1605-1687)

Verses upon his Divine Poesy

The soul's dark cottage, battered and decayed,
Lets in new light through chinks that time has made.
Stronger by weakness, wiser men become,
As they draw near to their eternal home.

On a Girdle

A narrow compass! and yet there
Dwelt all that's good, and all that's fair;
Give me but what this ribbon bound,
Take all the rest the sun goes round.

Go, lovely Rose

How small a part of time they share
That are so wondrous sweet and fair!

To a Lady, singing a Song of his composing

The eagle's fate and mine are one,
    Which, on the shaft that made him die,
Espied a feather of his own,
    Wherewith he wont to soar so high.

MILTON — (1608-1674)

Paradise Lost

Or if Sion hill
Delight thee more, and Siloa's brook, that flowed
Fast by the oracle of God.   Book i. Line 10

What in me is dark,
Illumine; what is low, raise and support;
That to the height of this great argument
I may assert eternal Providence,
And justify the ways of God to men. Book i. Line 22.

Yet from those flames
No light; but only darkness visible. Book i. Line 62.

Where peace
And rest can never dwell: hope never comes,
That comes to all. Book i. Line 65.

What though the field be lost?
All is not lost. Book i. Line 105.

The mind is its own place, and in itself
Can make a heaven of hell, a hell of heaven.
Book i. Line 254.

Here we may reign secure, and in my choice
To reign is worth ambition, though in hell:
Better to reign in hell than serve in heaven.
Book i. Line 261.

Heard so oft
In worst extremes and on the perilous edge
Of battle. Book i. Line 275.

Thick as autumnal leaves that strew the brooks
In Vallombrosa, where the Etrurian shades
High over-arched imbower. Book i. Line 303.

Awake, arise, or be for ever fallen! Book i. Line 330.
Sonorous metal blowing martial sounds. Book i. Line 540.
In perfect phalanx to the Dorian mood
Of flutes and soft recorders. Book i. Line 550.

Thrice he essayed, and thrice, in spite of scorn,
Tears, such as angels weep, burst forth. Book i. Line 619.

From morn
To noon he fell, from noon to dewy eve,
A summer's day. Book i. Line 742.

But all was false and hollow, though his tongue
Dropped manna; and could make the worse appear
The better reason, to perplex and dash
Maturest counsels. Book ii. Line 113.

With grave
Aspect he rose, and in his rising seemed
A pillar of state; deep on his front engraven
Deliberation sat and public care.   Book ii. Line 300.
With Atlantean shoulders, fit to bear
The weight of mightiest monarchies: his look
Drew audience and attention still as night
Or summer's noontide air.   Book ii. Line 306.
Fixed fate, free will, foreknowledge absolute.
                                        Book ii. Line 560.
The other shape,
If shape it might be called that shape had none
Distinguishable in member, joint, or limb.
                                        Book ii. Line 666.
Whence and what art thou, execrable shape?
                                        Book ii. Line 681.
And Death
Grinn'd horrible a ghastly smile, to hear
His famine should be filled.   Book ii. Line 846.
With ruin upon ruin, rout on rout,
Confusion worse confounded.   Book ii. Line 996.
Hail, holy light! offspring of Heaven first-born.
                                        Book iii. Line 1.
Or flocks, or herds, or human face divine.
                                        Book iii. Line 44.
Since called
The Paradise of Fools, to few unknown.
                                        Book iii. Line 495.
At whose sight all the stars
Hide their diminished heads.   Book iv. Line 34.

And in the lowest deep, a lower deep,
Still threatening to devour me, opens wide,
To which the hell I suffer seems a heaven.
                                        Book iv. Line 76.
So farewell hope, and with hope farewell fear,
Farewell remorse; all good to me is lost:
Evil, be thou my good.   Book iv. Line 108.
For contemplation he, and valor, formed,
For softness she, and sweet attractive grace.
                                        Book iv. Line 297.

His fair large front and eye sublime declared
Absolute rule; and hyacinthine locks
Round from his parted forelock manly hung
Clustering, but not beneath his shoulders broad.

Book iv. Line 300.

Imparadised in one another's arms.   Book iv. Line 506.

Now came still evening on, and twilight gray
Had in her sober livery all things clad.   Book iv. Line 598.

With thee conversing, I forget all time,
All seasons and their change, all please alike.

Book iv. Line 639.

Millions of spiritual creatures walk the earth
Unseen, both when we wake and when we sleep.

Book iv. Line 677.

Hail, wedded love, mysterious law; true source
Of human happiness.   Book iv. Line 750.

Not to know me argues yourselves unknown,
The lowest of your throng.   Book iv. Line 830.

Now morn, her rosy steps in the eastern clime
Advancing, sowed the earth with orient pearl.

Book v. Line 1.

Good, the more
Communicated, more abundant grows.   Book v. Line 71.

These are thy glorious works, Parent of good!

Book v. Line 153.

So saying, with despatchful look, in haste
She turns, on hospitable thoughts intent.   Book v. Line 331.

Thrones, dominations, princedoms, virtues, powers.

Book v. Line 601.

They eat, they drink, and in communion sweet
Quaff immortality and joy.   Book v. Line 637.

Dire was the noise
Of conflict.   Book vi. Line 211.

Still govern thou my song,
Urania, and fit audience find, though few.

Book vii. Line 30.

Cycle and epicycle, orb in orb.   Book viii. Line 84.

Grace was in all her steps, heaven in her eye,
In every gesture dignity and love.   Book viii. Line 488.

Her virtue and the conscience of her worth,
That would be wooed and not unsought be won.
Book viii. Line 502.

So well to know
Her own, that what she wills to do or say
Seems wisest, virtuousest, discreetest, best!
Book viii. Line 548.

Those graceful acts,
Those thousand decencies, that daily flow
From all her words and actions.   Book vii. Line 600.

To whom the angel, with a smile that glowed
Celestial rosy red (love's proper hue).
Book viii. Line 618.

For solitude sometimes is best society,
And short retirement urges sweet return.
Book ix. Line 249.

Yet I shall temper so
Justice with mercy, as may illustrate most
Them fully satisfied, and thee appease.   Book x. Line 77.

The world was all before them, where to choose
Their place of rest, and Providence their guide.
Book xii. Line 646.

PARADISE REGAINED

Athens, the eye of Greece, mother of arts
And eloquence.   Book iv. Line 240.
Thence to the famous orators repair,
Those ancient, whose resistless eloquence
Wielded at wild that fierce democraty,
Shook the arsenal, and fulmined over Greece,
To Macedon, and Artaxerxes' throne.
Book iv. Line 267.

As children gathering pebbles on the shore.
Book iv. Line 330.

SAMSON AGONISTES

Just are the ways of God,
And Justifiable to men.   Line 293.

He's gone, and who knows how he may report
Thy words, by adding fuel to the flame?   Line 1350.

COMUS

A thousand fantasies
Begin to throng into my memory,
Of calling shapes and beckoning shadows dire,
And airy tongues, that syllable men's names
On sands, and shores, and desert wildernesses.

                                                   Line 205.

Was I deceived, or did a sable cloud
Turn forth her silver lining on the night?   Line 221.
Can any mortal mixture of earth's mould
Breathe such divine, enchanting ravishment?   Line 244.
Who, as they sung, would take the prisoned soul
And lap it in Elysium.   Line 256.
He that has light within his own clear breast
May sit i' th' centre and enjoy bright day;
But he that hides a dark soul and foul thoughts
Benighted walks under the mid-day sun.   Line 381.
How charming is divine philosophy!
Not harsh and crabbed, as dull fools suppose;
But musical as is Apollo's lute,
And a perpetual feast of nectared sweets,
Where no crude surfeit reigns.   Line 476.
                I was all ear,
And took in strains that might create a soul
Under the ribs of Death.   Line 560.

LYCIDAS

He knew
Himself to sing, and build the lofty rhyme.   Line 10.
Without the meed of some melodious tear.   Line 14.
Fame is the spur that the clear spirit doth raise
(That last infirmity of noble minds)
To scorn delights and live laborious days;
But the fair guerdon when we hope to find,
And think to burst out into sudden blaze,
Comes the blind Fury with the abhorred shears,
And slits the thin-spun life.   Line 70.

Built in the eclipse and rigged with curses dark.   Line 101.
The pilot of the Galilean lake.   Line 109.
So sinks the day-star in the ocean bed,
And yet anon repairs his drooping head,
And tricks his beams, and with new spangled ore
Flames in the forehead of the morning sky.   Line 168.
To-morrow to fresh woods and pastures new.   Line 193.

L' ALLEGRO

Quips and cranks, and wanton wiles,
Nods and becks, and wreathed smiles.   Line 27.
Come, and trip it as you go,
On the light, fantastic toe.   Line 33.
And every shepherd tells his tale
Under the hawthorn in the dale.   Line 67.
Where perhaps some beauty lies,
The Cynosure of neighboring eyes.   Line 79.
Towered cities please us then,
And the busy hum of men.   Line 117.
Or sweetest Shakespeare, Fancy's child,
Warble his native wood-notes wild.   Line 133.
Lap me in soft Lydian airs,
Married to immortal verse,
Such as the meeting soul may pierce
In notes, with many a winding bout
Of linked sweetness long drawn out.   Line 136.

IL PENSEROSO

And looks commercing with the skies,
Thy rapt soul sitting in thine eyes.   Line 39.
Sweet bird, that shunn'st the noise of folly,
Most musical, most melancholy!   Line 61.
Such notes, as, warbled to the string,
Drew iron tears down Pluto's cheek.   Line 106.
Where more is meant than meets the ear.   Line 120.
And storied windows richly dight,
Casting a dim, religious light.   Line 159

Sonnet to the Lady Margaret Ley

That old man eloquent.

Sonnet on his Blindness

They also serve who only stand and wait.

Second Sonnet to Cyriac Skinner

Yet I argue not
Against Heaven's hand or will, nor bate a jot
Of heart or hope; but still bear up and steer
Right onward.

Sonnet on his Deceased Wife

But oh! as to embrace me she inclined,
I waked; she fled; and day brought back my night.

SAMUEL BUTLER — (1612-1680)

Hudibras

Besides, 't is known he could speak Greek
As naturally as pigs squeak.   Part i. Canto i. Line 51.
He could distinguish, and divide
A hair, 'twixt south and southwest side.
                              Part i. Canto i. Line 67.
For rhetoric, he could not ope
His mouth, but out there flew a trope.
                              Part i. Canto i. Line 81.
Whatever sceptic could inquire for,
For every why he had a wherefore.
                              Part i. Canto i. Line 131.
He knew what 's what, and that 's as high
As metaphysic wit can fly.   Part i. Canto i. Line 149.
And prove their doctrine orthodox,
By Apostolic blows and knocks.   Part i. Canto i. Line 199.
Compound for sins they are inclined to,
By damning those they have no mind to.
                              Part i. Canto i. Line 215.

For rhyme the rudder is of verses,
With which, like ships, they steer their courses.
> Part i. Canto i. Line 463.

He ne'er considered it, as loth
To look a gift-horse in the mouth.
> Part i. Canto i. Line 489.

Quoth Hudibras, "I smell a rat;
Ralpho, thou dost prevaricate."
> Part i. Canto i. Line 821.

Or shear swine, all cry and no wool.
> Part i. Canto i. Line 852.

And bid the devil take the hin'most,
Which at this race is like to win most.
> Part i. Canto ii. Line 633.

With many a stiff thwack, many a bang,
Hard crab-tree and old iron rang.
> Part i. Canto ii. Line 831.

Ay me! what perils do environ
The man that meddles with cold iron.
> Part i. Canto iii. Line 1.

Nor do I know what is become
Of him, more than the Pope of Rome.
> Part i. Canto iii. Line 263.

H' had got a hurt
O' th' inside of a deadlier sort.
> Part i. Canto iii. Line 309.

I am not now in fortune's power;
He that is down can fall no lower.
> Part i. Canto iii. Line 877.

Thou hast
Outrun the Constable at last.
> Part i. Canto iii. Line 1367.

For one for sense, and one for rhyme,
I think's sufficient at one time.   Part ii. Canto i. Line 29.

For what is worth in anything,
But so much money as 't will bring.
> Part ii. Canto i. Line 465.

The sun had long since in the lap
Of Thetis taken out his nap,

And, like a lobster boiled, the morn
From black to red began to turn.

Part ii. Canto ii. Line 29

Have always been at daggers-drawing,
And one another clapper-clawing.

Part ii. Canto ii. Line 79.

And look before you ere you leap;
For as you sow, y' are like to reap.

Part ii. Canto ii. Line 503.

Doubtless the pleasure is as great
Of being cheated, as to cheat.   Part ii. Canto iii. Line 1.

He made an instrument to know
If the moon shine at full or no.

.   .   .   .   .   .

And prove that she's not made of green cheese.*

Part ii. Canto iii. Line 261.

You have a wrong sow by the ear.

Part ii. Canto iii. Line 580.

To swallow gudgeons ere they're catched,
And count their chickens ere they're hatched.
As quick as lightning, in the breach
Just in the place where honor 's lodged,
As wise philosophers have judged,
Because a kick in that place more
Hurts honor than deep wounds before.

Part ii. Canto iii. Line 1067.

As he that has two strings t' his bow.

Part iii. Canto i. Line 3.

True as the dial to the sun,
Although it be not shined upon.

Part iii. Canto ii. Line 175.

For those that fly may fight again,
Which he can never do that 's slain.

Part iii. Canto iii. Line 243.

He that complies against his will
Is of his own opinion still.   Part iii. Canto iii. Line 547.

---

* "The moon is made of a green cheese."
Jack Jugler, p. 46.

MARQUIS OF MONTROSE — (1612-1650)

Song, "My Dear and only Love."

I'll make thee famous by my pen,
And glorious by my sword.

DRYDEN — (1631-1700)

Alexander's Feast

None but the brave deserves the fair.	Line 15.
Sweet is pleasure after pain.	Line 60.

Soothed with the sound, the king grew vain;
Fought all his battles o'er again;
And thrice he routed all his foes; and thrice he slew the
    slain.   Line 66.

Fallen from his high estate,
And weltering in his blood;
Deserted, at his utmost need,
By those his former bounty fed;
On the bare 'earth exposed he lies,
With not a friend to close his eyes.   Line 78.

For pity melts the mind to love.   Line 96.

War, he sung, is toil and trouble;
Honor, but an empty bubble.   Line 99.

Take the good the gods provide thee.   Line 106.

Sighed and looked, and sighed again.   Line 120.

And, like another Helen, fired another Troy.   Line 154.
Could swell the soul to rage, or kindle soft desire.
                                                          Line 160.

He raised a mortal to the skies
She drew an angel down.   Line 169.

Cymon and Iphigenia

He trudged along, unknowing what he sought,
And whistled as he went, for want of thought.   Line 84.

Absalom and Achitophel

A fiery soul, which, working out its way,

Fretted the pigmy body to decay,
And o'er informed the tenement of clay.

Great wits are sure to madness near allied,
And thin partitions do their bounds divide.

Part i. Line 163.

Resolved to ruin or to rule the state.   Part i. Line 174.

Who think too little, and who talk too much.

Part i. Line 545.

A man so various, that he seemed to be
Not one, but all mankind's epitome;
Stiff in opinions, always in the wrong,
Was everything by starts, and nothing long.

Part i. Line 545.

Beware the fury of a patient man.   Part i. Line 1005

For every inch, that is not fool, is rogue.

Part ii. Line 463.

All for Love. Prologue

Errors like straws upon the surface flow;
He who would search for pearls must dive below.

Men are but children of a larger growth.   Act iv. Sc. 1.

I am as free as nature first made man,
Ere the base laws of servitude began,

When wild in woods the noble savage ran.

Conquest of Grenada. Part i. Sc. 1.

Spanish Friar

There is a pleasure
In being mad which none but madmen know.

Act ii. Sc. 1.

Don Sebastian

This is the porcelain clay of human kind.

Act i. Sc. 1.

Translation of Juvenal's 10th Satire

Look round the habitable world, how few
Know their own good, or, knowing it, pursue.

Prologue to Lee's Sophonisba

Thespis, the first professor of our art,
At country wakes sung ballads from a cart.

Imitation of the 29th of Horace

Happy the man, and happy he alone,
He, who can call to-day his own:
He who, secure within, can say,
To-morrow do thy worst, for I have lived to-day.

On Milton

Three Poets, in three distant ages born,
Greece, Italy, and England did adorn;
The first in loftiness of thought surpassed,
The next in majesty, in both the last.
The force of nature could no further go;
To make a third she joined the other two.

JOHN BUNYAN — (1628-1688)

Apology for his Book

And so I penned
It down, until at last it came to be,
For length and breadth, the bigness which you see.

Some said, "John, print it," others said, "Not so."
Some said, "It might do good," others said, "No."

Pilgrim's Progress

The Slough of Despond.

EARL OF ROSCOMMON — (1633-1684)

Essay on Translated Verse

Immodest words admit of no defence,
For want of decency is want of sense.

When vice prevails, and impious men bear sway,
The post of honor is a private station.   Act. v. Sc. **1.**
It must be so. — Plato, thou reasonest well.
Else whence this pleasing hope, this fond desire,
This longing after immortality?

          .   .   .   .   .

'T is the Divinity that stirs within us;
'T is Heaven itself that points out an hereafter,
And intimates Eternity to man.   Act v. Sc. **1.**
I'm weary of conjectures.   Act v. Sc. **1.**
The soul secured in her existence, smiles
At the drawn dagger, and defies its point.

          Act v. Sc. **1.**

The wreck of matter, and the crush of worlds.

          Act v. Sc. **1.**

The Campaign

And, pleased th' Almighty's orders to perform,
Rides in the whirlwind and directs the storm.*

From the Letter on Italy

For wheresoe'er I turn my ravished eyes,
Gay gilded scenes and shining prospects rise;
Poetic fields encompass me around,
And still I seem to tread on classic ground.**

Ode

The spacious firmament on high,
With all the blue, ethereal sky,
And spangled heavens, a shining frame,

---

* This line has been frequently ascribed to Pope, as it is
found in the Dunciad, Book iii. line 261.

** Malone states that this was the first time the phrase *classic
ground,* since so common, was ever used.

Their great Original proclaim.

Soon as the evening shades prevail,
The moon takes up the wondrous tale,
And nightly to the listening earth
Repeats the story of her birth;
While all the stars that round her burn,
And all the planets in their turn,
Confirm the tidings as they roll,
And spread the truth from pole to pole.

For ever singing, as they shine,
The hand that made us is divine.

JONATHAN SWIFT — (1667-1745)

I've often wished that I had clear,
For life, six hundred pounds a year,
A handsome house to lodge a friend,
A river at my garden's end.
> *Imitation of Horace.* B. ii. Sat. **6.**

Poetry, a Rhapsody

So geographers, in Afric maps,
With savage pictures fill their gaps,
And o'er unhabitable downs
Place elephants for want of towns.

WILLIAM CONGREVE — (1669-1729)

The Mourning Bride

Music hath charms to soothe the savage breast,
To soften rocks, or bend a knotted oak.

By magic numbers and persuasive sound.
> Act i. Sc. **1.**

Heaven has no rage like love to hatred turned,
Nor Hell a fury like a woman scorned.
> Act iii. Sc. **1.**

ALEXANDER POPE — (1688-1744)

Essay on Man

Expatiate free o'er all this scene of man;
A mighty maze! but not without a plan. Epistle i. Line 5.
Eye nature's walks, shoot folly as it flies,
And catch the manners living as they rise. Line 13.
A hero perish or a sparrow fall. Line 88.
Hope springs eternal in the human breast:
Man never *is*, but always *to be* blest. Line 95.
Lo, the poor Indian! whose untutored mind
Sees God in clouds, or hears him in the wind.

Line 99.
Die of a rose in aromatic pain? Line 200.
One truth is clear, Whatever is, is right. Line 294.
Know then thyself, presume not God to scan;

Epistle ii. Line 1.
The proper study of mankind is man.*
Vice is a monster of so frightful mien,
As to be hated, needs but to be seen;
But seen too oft, familiar with her face,
We first endure, then pity, then embrace.

Line 217.
Virtuous and vicious every man must be,
Few in th' extreme, but all in the degree. Line 231.
Pleased with a rattle, tickled with a straw. Line 276.
For modes of faith let graceless zealots fight;
His can't be wrong whose life is in the right.

Epistle iii. Line 305.
Order is Heaven's first law. Epistle iv. Line 49.
Honor and shame from no condition rise;
Act well your part, — there all the honor lies.

Line 193.
Worth makes the man, and want of it the fellow;
The rest is all but leather on prunella. Line 203.

---

* From Charron (de la Sagesse): — "La vraye science et le vray etude de l'homme c'est l'homme."

What can ennoble sots, or slaves, or cowards?
Alas! not all the blood of all the Howards.   Line 215.
A wit's a feather, and a chief a rod;
An honest man 's the noblest work of God.   Line 247.
Plays round the head, but comes not to the heart.
                                             Line 254.

        Think how Bacon shined,
The wisest, brightest, meanest of mankind.   Line 281.
Virtue alone is happiness below.   Line 310.
Slave to no sect, who takes no private road,
But looks through nature up to nature's God. Line 330.
Formed by thy converse happily to steer
From grave to gay, from lively to severe.   Line 379.

MORAL ESSAYS

'T is from high life high characters are drawn, —
A saint in crape is twice a saint in lawn.
                                    Epistle i. Line 135.
'T is education forms the common mind:
Just as the twig is bent, the tree's inclined.
                                             Line 149.

Odious! in woollen! 't would a saint provoke,
Were the last words that poor Narcissa spoke.
                                             Line 246.

Whether the charmers sinner it or saint it,
If folly grow romantic, I must paint it.
                                    Epistle ii. Line 15.
Fine by defect and delicately weak.   Line 43.
With too much quickness ever to be taught,
With too much thinking to have common thought.
                                             Line 97.

Men, some to business, some to pleasure take;
But every woman is at heart a rake.   Line 215.
And mistress of herself, though china fall.   Line 268.
Woman's at best a contradiction still.   Line 270.
Who shall decide when doctors disagree?
                                    Epistle iii. Line 1.
But thousands die without or this or that,
Die, and endow a college or a cat.   Line 95.

The ruling passion, be it what it will,
The ruling passion conquers reason still.   Line 153.
Extremes in nature equal good produce.   Line 161.
Rise, honest muse! and sing, — The man of Ross.
                                            Line 250.
Who builds a church to God, and not to fame,
Will never mark the marble with his name.   Line 285.

AN ESSAY ON CRITICISM

'T is with our judgements as our watches; none
Go just alike, yet each believes his own.   Part 1. Line 9.
And snatch a grace beyond the reach of art.   Line 153.
A little learning is a dangerous thing.
Drink deep, or taste not the Pierian spring.
                                    Part ii. Line 215.
Hills peep o'er hills, and Alps on Alps arise.   Line 232.
True wit is nature to advantage dressed,
What oft was thought, but ne'er so well expressed.
                                            Line 297.
That, like a wounded snake, drags its slow length along.
                                            Line 357.
True ease in writing comes from art, not chance,
As those move easiest who have learned to dance.
                                            Line 362.
The sound must seem an echo to the sense.   Line 365.
To err is human: to forgive, divine.   Line 525.
For fools rush in where angels fear to tread.
                                    Part iii. Line 625.

ELEGY TO THE MEMORY OF AN
UNFORTUNATE LADY

By strangers honored and by strangers mourned.
        .   .   .   .   .
And bear about the mockery of woe
To midnight dances and the public show.   Line 54.

THE RAPE OF THE LOCK

On her white breast a sparkling cross she wore,
Which Jews might kiss and infidels adore.

Canto ii. Line 7.

If to her share some female errors fall,
Look on her face, and you'll forget them all.

Canto ii. Line 17.

At every word a reputation dies.   Canto ii. Line 16.

The hungry judges soon the sentence sign,
And wretches hang, that jurymen may dine.   Line 21.

SATIRES AND IMITATIONS OF HORACE.

Shut, shut the door, good John.   Prologue, Line 1.

E'en Sunday shines no Sabbath day to me.   Line 12.

Who pens a stanza when he should engross.   Line 18.

As yet a child, nor yet a fool to fame,
I lisped in numbers, for the numbers came.   Line 127.

Should such a man, too fond to rule alone,
Bear, like the Turk, no brother near the throne.   Line 197.

Damn with faint praise, assent with civil leer,
And without sneering teach the rest to sneer.   Line 201.

Who breaks a butterfly upon a wheel?   Line 308.

Wit that can creep, and pride that licks the dust.

Line 333.

Lord Fanny spins a thousand such a day.

Book ii. Satire i. Line 6.

Satire 's my weapon, but I'm too discreet
To run a muck, and tilt at all I meet.   Line 69.

Then St. John mingles with my friendly bowl,
The feast of reason and the flow of soul.   Line 127.

For I, who hold sage Homer's rule the best,
Welcome the coming, speed the going guest.*
The mob of gentlemen who wrote with ease.

Book ii. Epistle i. Line 108.

Epilogue to the Satires

Do good by stealth, and blush to find it fame.

Dialogue i. Line 136.

---

* See the Odyssey, Book xv. line 83.

Epitaph on Gay

Of manners gentle, of affections mild;
In wit a man, simplicity a child.

THE DUNCIAD

And solid pudding against empty praise.   Book i. Line 54.
All crowd, who foremost shall be damned to fame.
                                        Book iii. Line 165.
Silence, ye wolves! while Ralph to Cynthia howls,
And makes night hideous; — answer him, ye owls.
E'en Palinurus nodded at the helm.   Book iv. Line 614.

ODYSSEY

          Few sons attain the praise
Of their great sires, and most their sires disgrace.
                                        Book ii. Line 315.
Far from gay cities and the ways of men.
                                        Book xiv. Line 410.
Who love too much, hate in the like extreme.
                                        Book xv. Line 79.
True friendship's laws are by this rule expressed,
Welcome the coming, speed the parting guest.
                                        Book xv. Line 83.

Windsor Forest

Thus, if small things we may with great compare.

Martinus Scriblerus on the Art of Sinking in Poetry

Ye Gods! annihilate but space and time,
And make two lovers happy.   Chapter xi.

Epitaph on the Hon. S. Harcourt

Who ne'er knew joy but friendship might divide,
Or gave his father grief but when he died.

THOMAS TICKELL — (1686-1740)

On the Death of Addison

Nor e'er was to the bowers of bliss conveyed
A fairer spirit, or more welcome shade.   Line 45.
There taught us how to live; and (oh! too high
The price for knowledge) taught us how to die.

Colin and Lucy

I hear a voice you cannot hear,
    Which says I must not stay,
I see a hand you cannot see,
    Which beckons me away.

JOHN GAY — (1688-1732)

What D' ye Call 't.

So comes a reckoning when the banquet 's o'er,
The dreadful reckoning, and men smile no more.
                                        Act ii. Sc. 9.

Beggars' Opera

O'er the hills and far away.

How happy could I be with either,
Were 't other dear charmer away.   Act i. Sc. 1.

FABLES

The Shepherd and the Philosopher

Whence is thy learning? Hath thy toil
O'er books consumed the midnight oil?

The Mother, the Nurse, and the Fairy

When yet was ever found a mother
Who 'd give her booby for another?

The Sick Man and the Angel

While there is life there 's hope, he cried.

The Hare and many Friends

And when a lady 's in the case,
You know all other things give place.

Epitaph on Himself

Life 's a jest, and all things show it;
I thought so once, and now I know it.

LADY MARY WORTLEY MONTAGUE
(1690-1762)

The Lady's Resolve

Let this great maxim be my virtue's guide, —
In part she is to blame that has been tried;
He comes too near, that comes to be denied.

NICHOLAS ROWE — (1673-1718)

The Fair Penitent

Is she not more than painting can express,
Or youthful poets fancy when they love?
Is this that gallant, gay Lothario?   Act v. Sc. 1.

JOHN PHILIPS — (1676-1708)

My galligaskins, that have long withstood
The winter's fury and encroaching frosts,
By time subdued, (what will not time subdue!)
A horrid chasm disclosed.
Splendid Shilling. Line 121.

THOMAS PARNELL — (1679-1718)

Remote from men, with God he passed his days,
Prayer all his business, all his pleasure praise.
The Hermit. Line 5.

BARTON BOOTH — (1681-1733)

Song

True as the needle to the pole,
Or as the dial to the sun.

MATTHEW GREEN — (1696-1737)

The Spleen

Fling but a stone, the giant dies.   **Line 93.**

JOHN BYROM — (1691-1763)

On the Feuds between Handel and Bononcini.*

Some say, compared to Bononcini,
That Mynheer Handel 's but a ninny;
Others aver that he to Handel
Is scarcely fit to hold a candle.
Strange all this difference should be
'Twist Tweedledum and Tweedledee.

The Astrologer

As clear as a whistle.

Epigram on Two Monopolists

Bone and skin, two millers thin,
    Would starve us all, or near it;
But be it known to Skin and Bone
    That Flesh and Blood can 't bear it.

---

* "Nourse asked me if I had seen the verses upon Handel and Bononcini, not knowing that they were mine." Byrom's Remains (Cheltenham Soc.), Vol. I. p. 173. The last two lines have been attributed to Swift and Pope. *Vide* Scott's edition of Swift, and Dyce's edition of Pope.

BISHOP BERKELEY — (1684-1753)

On the Prospect of Planting Arts and Learning in America

Westward the course of empire takes its way;
   The four first acts already past,
A fifth shall close the drama with the day;
   Time's noblest offspring is the last.

ROBERT BLAIR — (1699-1746)

The good he scorned,

Stalked off reluctant, like an ill-used ghost,
Not to return; or if it did, in visits
Like those of angels, short and far between.
                The Grave. Part ii. Line 586.

EDWARD YOUNG — (1681-1765)

NIGHT THOUGHTS

Tired Nature's sweet restorer, balmy sleep!
                         Night i. Line 1.
The bell strikes one. We take no note of time
But from its loss.   Night i. Line 55.
To waft a feather or to drown a fly.   Night i. Line 154.
Be wise to-day; 't is madness to defer.   Night i. Line 390.
Procrastination is the thief of time.   Night i. Line 393.
At thirty man suspects himself a fool;
Knows it at forty, and reforms his plan.
                        Night i. Line 417.
All men think all men mortal but themselves.
                        Night i. Line 424.
'T is greatly wise to talk with our past hours,
And ask them what report they bore to heaven.
                        Night ii. Line 376.
How blessings brighten as they take their flight!
                        Night ii. Line 602.

The chamber where the good man meets his fate
Is privileged beyond the common walk
Of virtuous life, quite in the verge of heaven.
Night ii. Line 633.

Beautiful as sweet!
And young as beautiful! and soft as young!
And gay as soft! and innocent as gay!
Night iii. Line 81.

Lovely in death the beauteous ruin lay.
Night iii. Line 104.

The knell, the shroud, the mattock, and the grave,
The deep, damp vault, the darkness, and the worm.
Night iv. Line 10.

Man makes a death, which nature never made.
Night iv. Line 15.

Man wants but little, nor that little long.
Night iv. Line 118.

The man of wisdom is the man of years.
Night v. Line 775.

Death loves a shining mark, a signal blow.
Night v. Line 1011.

Pigmies are pigmies still, though perched on Alps,
And pyramids are pyramids in vales.
Night vi. Line 309.

And all may do what has by man been done.
Night vi. Line 606.

The man that blushes is not quite a brute.
Night vii. Line 496.

An undevout astronomer is mad.
Night ix. Line 771.

Emblazed to seize the sight; who runs, may read.
Night ix. Line 1660.

LOVE OF FAME

Some, for renown, on scraps of learning dote,
And think they grow immortal as they quote.
Satire i. Line 89.

None think the great unhappy, but the great.
Satire i. Line 238.

Where nature's end of language is declined,
And men talk only to conceal their mind.*
Satire ii. Line 207.
How commentators each dark passage shun,
And hold their farthing candle to the sun.**
Satire vii. Line 97.

Lines Written with the Diamond Pencil of Lord Chesterfield

Accept a miracle, instead of wit,
See two dull lines with Stanhope's pencil writ.

HENRY CAREY — (1663-1743)

God save the King.***

God save our gracious king,
Long live our noble king,
God save the king.

To thee, and gentle Rigdum Funnidos,
Our gratulations flow in streams unbounded.
Chrononhotonthologos. Act i. Sc. 3.
Go call a coach, and let a coach be called,
And let the man who calleth be the caller;
And in his calling let him nothing call
But Coach! Coach! Coach! O for a coach, ye gods!
Act ii. Sc. 4.

---

* "Ils n'emploient les paroles que pour déguiser leurs pensées." — *Voltaire.*

** Imitated by Crabbe in the Parish Register, Part I, Introduction, and taken originally from Burton's Anatomy of Melancholy, Part III. Sec. 2 Mem. 1. Subs. 2. "But to enlarge or illustrate this power or effects of love is to set a candle in the sun."

*** The authorship both of the words and music of "God save the King" has long been a matter of dispute, and is still unsettled, though the weight of the evidence is in favor of Carey's claim.

ISAAC WATTS — (1674-1748)

DIVINE SONGS

To God the Father, God the Son,
    And God the Spirit, three in one,
Be honor, praise, and glory given,
    By all on earth, and all in heaven.

Hush! my dear, lie still and slumber;
    Holy angels guard thy bed!
Heavenly blessings without number
    Gently falling on thy head.

Let dogs delight to bark and bite
    For God hath made them so;
Let bears and lions growl and fight,
    For 't is their nature too.

How doth the little busy bee
    Improve each shining hour,
And gather honey all the day,
    From every opening flower.

Hark! from the tombs a doleful sound.
'T is the voice of the sluggard, I heard him complain,
"You have waked me too soon, I must slumber again."

SIR SAMUEL TUKE — (-1673)

Adventures of Five Hours

He is a fool who thinks by force or skill
To turn the current of a woman's will.

                                 Act v. Sc. 3.

AARON HILL — (1685-1750)

Epilogue to Zara

First, then, a woman will, or won't, — depend on 't;
If she will do 't, she will; and there 's an end on 't.

But, if she won't, since safe and sound your trust is,
Fear is affront: and jealousy injustice.*

Verses Written on a Window in Scotland

Tender-handed stroke a nettle,
　　And it stings you for your pains;
Grasp it like a man of mettle,
　　And it soft as silk remains.

'T is the same with common natures:
　　Use 'em kindly, they rebel;
But be rough as nutmeg-graters,
　　And the rogues obey you well.

RICHARD SAVAGE — (1698-1743)

He lives to build, not boast a generous race:
No tenth transmitter of a foolish face.

The Bastard. Line 7.

JAMES THOMSON — (1700-1748)

THE SEASONS

Base envy withers at another's joy,
And hates that excellence it cannot reach.

Spring. Line 283.

　　　　　But who can paint
Like Nature? Can imagination boast,
Amid its gay creation, hues like hers?

Line 465.

Delightful task! to rear the tender thought,
To teach the young idea how to shoot.

Line 1149.

---

* The following lines are copied from the pillar erected on
the mount in the Dane John Field, Canterbury: —

"Where is the man who has the power and skill
To stem the torrent of a woman's will?
For if she will, she will, you may depend on 't;
And if she won't, she won't; so there's an end on 't."

An elegant sufficiency, content,
Retirement, rural quiet, friendship, books,
Ease and alternate labor, useful life,
Progressive virtue, and approving Heaven!

Line 1158.

Sighed and looked unutterable things.

Summer. Line 1188.

A lucky chance, that oft decides the fate
Of mighty monarchs.

Line 1285.

So stands the statue that enchants the world.

Line 1346.

Loveliness
Needs not the foreign aid of ornament,
But is when unadorned, adorned the most.

Autumn. Line 204.

For still the world prevailed, and its dread laugh,
Which scarce the firm philosopher can scorn.

Line 233.

Cruel as death, and hungry as the grave.

Winter. Line 393.

Shade, unperceived, so softening into shade.

Hymn. Line 25.

From seeming evil still educing good.   Line 114.

Come then, expressive silence, muse his praise.

Line 118.

A little round, fat, oily man of God.

Castle of Indolence. Canto i. St. 69.

Rule Britannia, Britannia rules the waves;
Britons never will be slaves.

Alfred. Act ii. Sc. 5.

For ever, Fortune, wilt thou prove
An unrelenting foe to love;
And, when we meet a mutual heart,
Step rudely in, and bid us part?
Song, "For ever, Fortune."
O Sophonisba! Sophonisba, O!*

Sophonisba. Act iii. Sc. 2.

* This line was altered, after the second edition, to
"O Sophonisba! I am wholly thine."

JOHN DYER — (1700-1758)

Ever charming, ever new,
When will the landscape tire the view.
Grongar Hill. Line 103.

As yon summit soft and fair,
Clad in colors of the air,
Which to those who journey near
Barren, brown, and rough appear.

Line 123.

PHILIP DODDRIDGE — (1702-1751)

Epigram on his Family Arms

Live while you live, the epicure would say,
And seize the pleasures of the present day;
Live while you live, the sacred preacher cries,
And give to God each moment as it flies.
Lord, in my views let both united be;
I live in pleasure, when I live to thee.

ROBERT DODSLEY — (1703-1764)

The Parting Kiss

One kind kiss before we part,
Drop a tear and bid adieu;
Though we sever, my fond heart
Till we meet shall pant for you.

SAMUEL JOHNSON — (1709-1784)

Prologue on the Opening of Drury Lane Theatre

Each change of many-colored life he drew,
Exhausted worlds, and then imagined new.

.   .   .   .   .

And panting time toiled after him in vain.

.   .   .   .   .

For we that live to please must please to live.

Vanity of Human Wishes

Let observation with extensive view
Survey mankind, from China to Peru.*
Line 1.

There mark what ills the scholar's life assail, —
Toil, envy, want, the patron, and the jail.
Line 159.

He left the name, at which the world grew pale,
To point a moral, or adorn a tale.   Line 221.

Hides from himself his state, and shuns to know
That life protracted is protracted woe.   Line 257.

Superfluous lags the veteran on the stage.   Line 308.

And Swift, expires, a driveller and a show.   Line 318.

Roll darkling down the torrent of his fate.
Line 346.

Of all the griefs that harass the distressed,
Sure the most bitter is a scornful jest.
London. Line 166.

This mournful truth is everywhere confessed,
Slow rises worth by poverty depressed.

Lines added to Goldsmith's Traveller

How small, of all that human hearts endure,
That part which laws or kings can cause or cure!
Still to ourselves in every place consigned,
Our own felicity we make or find.
With secret course, which no loud storms annoy,
Glides the smooth current of domestic joy.

Line added to Goldsmith's Deserted Village

Trade's proud empire hastes to swift decay.

*From Dr. Madden's "Boulter's Monument." Supposed
to have been inserted by Dr. Johnson. 1745.*

Words are men's daughters, but God's sons are things.

---

* The Universal Love of Pleasure, line 1: —
    "All human race, from China to Peru,
    Pleasure, howe'er disguised by art, pursue."
Rev. Thos. Warton.

Ye who listen with credulity to the whispers of fancy, and pursue with eagerness the phantoms of hope; who expect that age will perform the promises of youth, and that the deficiencies of the present day will be supplied by the morrow; attend to the history of Rasselas, Prince of Abyssinia.   Rasselas. Chapter i.

Epitaph on Robert Levett

In Misery's darkest cavern known,
    His useful care was ever high,
Where hopeless Anguish poured his groan,
    And lonely Want retired to die.

Epitaph on Claudius Phillips, the Musician

Phillips, whose touch harmonious could remove
The pangs of guilty power or hapless love;
Rest here, distressed by poverty no more,
Here find that calm thou gav'st so oft before;
Sleep, undisturbed, within this peaceful shrine,
Till angels wake thee with a note like thine.

LORD LYTTELTON — (1709-1773)

Prologue to Thomson's Coriolanus

For his chaste Muse employed her heaven-taught lyre
None but the noblest passions to inspire,
Not one immoral, one corrupted thought,
One line, which dying he could wish to blot.

Epigram

None without hope e'er loved the brightest fair;
But love can hope where reason would despair.

Soliloquy on a Beauty in the Country

Where none admire, 't is useless to excel;
Where none are beaux, 't is vain to be a belle.

Song

Alas! by some degree of woe
  We every bliss must gain;
The heart can ne'er a transport know,
  That never feels a pain.

EDWARD MOORE — (1712-1757)

Fable IX. The Farmer, the Spaniel, and the Cat.

Can't I another's face commend,
And to her virtues be a friend,
But instantly your forehead lowers,
As if *her* merit lessened *yours?*

Fable X. The Spider and the Bee

The maid who modestly conceals
Her beauties, while she hides, reveals;
Give but a glimpse, and fancy draws
Whate'er the Grecian Venus was.

.   .   .   .   .

But from the hoop 's bewitching round,
Her very shoe has power to wound.

The Happy Marriage

Time still, as he flies, adds increase to her truth,
And gives to her mind what he steals from her youth.

'T is now the summer of your youth: time has not cropt
the roses from your cheek, though sorrow long has washed
them.

The Gamester. Act iii. Sc. 4.

WILLIAM SHENSTONE — (1714-1763)

Written on the Window of an Inn

Whoe'er has travelled life's dull round
  Where'er his stages may have been,

May sigh to think he still has found
His warmest welcome at an inn.

Jemmy Dawson

For seldom shall you hear a tale
So sad, so tender, and so true.

The Schoolmistress

Her cap, far whiter than the driven snow,
Emblems right meet of decency does yield.

JOHN BROWN — (1715-1766)

Now let us thank the Eternal Power: convinced
That Heaven but tries our virtue by affliction,
That oft the cloud which wraps the present hour
Serves but to brighten all our future days.

Barbarossa. Act v. Sc. 3.

DAVID GARRICK — (1716-1779)

Prologue on Quitting the Stage in 1776, 10th June

Their cause I plead, — plead it in heart and mind;
A fellow-feeling makes one wondrous kind.

On the Death of Mr. Pelham

Let others hail the rising sun:
I bow to that whose race is run.

THOMAS GRAY — (1716-1771)

On a Distant Prospect of Eton College

Ah, happy hills! ah, pleasing shade!
Ah, fields beloved in vain!
Where once my careless childhood strayed,
A stranger yet to pain!

Alas! regardless of their doom,
The little victims play;

No sense have they of ills to come,
Nor care beyond to-day.

No more: where ignorance is bliss,
'T is folly to be wise.

Progress of Poesy

O'er her warm cheek and rising bosom move
The bloom of young Desire, and purple light of Love

Ope the sacred source of sympathetic tears.

Thoughts that breathe, and words that burn.

The Bard

Give ample room, and verge enough.
Youth at the prow, and Pleasure at the helm.

Elegy in a Country Churchyard

The rude forefathers of the hamlet sleep.

The short and simple annals of the poor.

The paths of glory lead but to the grave.

Where through the long-drawn aisle and fretted vault
The pealing anthem swells the note of praise.

Hands, that the rod of empire might have swayed,
Or waked to ecstasy the living lyre.

Full many a flower is born to blush unseen,
And waste its sweetness on the desert air.

Some mute, inglorious Milton here may rest.

And read their history in a nation's eyes.

Forbade to wade through slaughter to a throne,
And shut the gates of mercy on mankind.

Along the cool, sequestered vale of life
They kept the noiseless tenor of their way.

Implores the passing tribute of a sigh.

And many a holy text around she strews,
That teach the rustic moralist to die.

Nor cast one longing, lingering look behind.

E'en from the tomb the voice of nature cries,
E'en in our ashes, live their wonted fires.

A youth, to fortune and to fame unknown.

Large was his bounty, and his soul sincere.

He gave to misery (all he had) a tear.

The bosom of his Father and his God.

Ode on the Pleasure arising from Vicissitude

The meanest floweret of the vale,
The simplest note that swells the gale,
The common sun, the air, the skies,
To him are opening paradise.

WILLIAM COLLINS — (1720-1756)

Ode in 1746

How sleep the brave, who sink to rest,
By all their country's wishes blessed!

By fairy hands their knell is rung;

By forms unseen their dirge is sung;
There Honor comes, a pilgrim gray,
To bless the turf that wraps their clay;
And Freedom shall awhile repair,
To dwell a weeping hermit there.
When Music, heavenly maid, was young,
While yet in early Greece she sung.

The Passions. Line 1.

Filled with fury, rapt, inspired.   Line 10.

'T was sad by fits, by starts 't was wild.   Line 28.

In notes by distance made more sweet.   Line 6C.

In hollow murmurs died away.   Line 68.

O Music! sphere-descended maid,
Friend of pleasure, wisdom's aid!   Line 95.

Well may your hearts believe the truths I tell;
'T is virtue makes the bliss, where'er we dwell.

Eclogue 1. Line 5.

Ode on the Death of Thomson

In yonder grave a Druid lies.

MARK AKENSIDE — (1721-1770)

Epistle to Curio

The man forget not, though in rags he lies,
And know the mortal through a crown's disguise.

NATHANIEL COTTON — (1721-1788)

If solid happiness we prize,
Within our breast this jewel lies;
    And they are fools who roam:
The world has nothing to bestow;
From our own selves our joys must flow,
    And that dear hut, — our home.

The Fireside. St. 3.

Thus hand in hand through life we'll go;
Its checkered paths of joy and woe
    With cautious steps we'll tread.

St. 13.

JOHN HOME — (1722-1808)

In the first days
Of my distracting grief, I found myself
As women wish to be who love their lords.

Douglas. Act i. Sc. 1.

My name is Norval; on the Grampian hills
My father fed his flocks.

Act ii. Sc. 1.

OLIVER GOLDSMITH — (1728-1774)

THE TRAVELLER

Remote, unfriended, melancholy, slow.   Line 1.

Where'er I roam, whatever realms to see,
My heart untravelled fondly turns to thee.

Line 7.

And learn the luxury of doing good.   Line 22.

Some fleeting good that mocks me with the view.

Line 26.

Such is the patriot's boast, where'er we roam,
His first, best country ever is at home.   Line 77

By sports like these are all his cares beguiled;
The sports of children satisfy the child.   Line 153.

But winter lingering chills the lap of May.   Line 172.

So the loud torrent, and the whirlwind's roar,
But bind him to his native mountains more.

Line 217.

Alike all ages: dames of ancient days
Have led their children through the mirthful maze;
And the gay grandsire, skilled in gestic lore,
Has frisked beneath the burden of threescore.

Line 251.

Pride in their port, defiance in their eye,
I see the lords of human kind pass by.

Line 327.

For just experience tells, in every soil,
That those that think must govern those that toil.

Line 372.

Laws grind the poor, and rich men rule the law.

Line 386.

Forced from their homes, a melancholy train.

Line 409.

THE DESERTED VILLAGE

For talking age and whispering lovers made.

Line 14.

Ill fares the land to hastening ills a prey,
Where wealth accumulates, and men decay.
Princes and lords may flourish, or may fade,
A breath can make them, as a breath has made;
But a bold peasantry, their country's pride,
When once destroyed, can never be supplied.

Line 51.

And his best riches, ignorance of wealth.   Line 62.

A youth of labor with an age of ease.   Line 100.

While resignation gently slopes the way, —
And, all his prospects brightening to the last,
His heaven commences ere the world be past.

Line 110.

And the loud laugh that spoke the vacant mind.

Line 122.

A man he was to all the country dear,
And passing rich with forty pounds a year.

Line 141.

Shouldered his crutch and showed how fields were won.

Line 158.

Careless their merits or their faults to scan,
His pity gave ere charity began.   Line 161.

And even his failings leaned to virtue's side.   Line 164.

Allured to brighter worlds, and led the way.   Line 170.

And fools who came to scoff remained to pray.   Line 180

And plucked his gown, to share the good man's smile.

Line 184.

Eternal sunshine settles on its head.   Line 192.

The village master taught his little school.   Line 196.

Full well the busy whisper, circling round,

Conveyed the dismal tidings when he frowned.   Line 203.
For even though vanquished, he could argue still;
While words of learned length and thundering sound
Amazed the gazing rustics ranged around;
And still they gazed, and still the wonder grew
That one small head could carry all he knew.   Line 212.
Contrived a double debt to pay.   Line 229.
One native charm than all the gloss of art.   Line 254.
The heart distrusting asks, if this be joy.   Line 264.
Her modest looks the cottage might adorn,
Sweet as the primrose peeps beneath the thorn.   Line 329.
O Luxury! thou cursed by Heaven's decree.   Line 385.

RETALIATION

Who mixed reason with pleasure and wisdom with mirth.
                                                Line 24.
Who, born for the universe, narrowed his mind,
And to party gave up what was meant for mankind.
                                                Line 31.
Though equal to all things, for all things unfit.   Line 37.
An abridgment of all that was pleasant in man.   Line 94.

VICAR OF WAKEFIELD

Man wants but little here below,
Nor wants that little long.
                    Chapter viii. *The Hermit.*

The man recovered of the bite,
The dog it was that died.
                    Chapter xvii. *Elegy on a Mad Dog.*

When lovely woman stoops to folly,
    And finds too late that men betray,
What charm can soothe her melancholy?
    What art can wash her guilt away?

The only art her guilt to cover,
    To hide her shame from every eye,
To give repentance to her lover,
    And wring his bosom, is — to die.
                              Chapter xxiv.

Elegy on Mrs. Mary Blaize

The king himself has followed her
When she has walked before.

TOBIAS SMOLLETT — (1721-1771)

Ode to Independence

Thy spirit, Independence, let me share;
  Lord of the lion heart and eagle eye,
Thy steps I follow with my bosom bare,
  Nor heed the storm that howls along the sky.

THOMAS PERCY — (1728-1811)

Reliques of English Poetry. The Baffled Knight

He that wold not when he might,
He shall not when he wolda.

The Friar of Orders Gray

Weep no more, lady, weep no more,
  Thy sorrow is in vain;
For violets plucked the sweetest showers
  Will ne'er make grow again.

Sigh no more, ladies, sigh no more,
  Men were deceivers ever;
One foot on sea, and one on shore,
  To one thing constant never.

From Byrd's Psalmes, Sonets, &c. 1588

My mind to me a kingdom is;
  Such perfect joy therein I find,
As far exceeds all earthly bliss
  That God and Nature hath assigned.
Though much I want that most would have,
Yet still my mind forbids to crave.

BEILBY PORTEUS — (1731-1808)

One murder makes a villain,
Millions a hero.   *Death, a Poem.* Line 154.

JAMES BEATTIE — (1735-1766)

Ah! who can tell how hard it is to climb
The steep where Fame's proud temple shines afar?
                        The Minstrel. Book i. St. 1.
He thought as a sage, but he felt as a man.
                        The Hermit. Line 8.

Epigram. The Bucks had dined

How hard their lot who neither won nor lost.

CHARLES CHURCHILL — (1741-1764)

But spite of all the criticising elves,
Those who would make us feel — must feel themselves.
                        The Rosciad. Line 861.

MRS. THRALE — (1740-1822)

Three Warnings

The tree of deepest root is found
Least willing still to quit the ground;
'T was therefore said, by ancient sages,
    That love of life increased with years
So much, that in our latter stages,
When pains grow sharp, and sickness rages,
The greatest love of life appears.

WILLIAM COWPER — (1731-1800)

THE TASK

God made the country, and man made the town.*
                        Book i. *The Sofa.*

---

* "God the first garden made, and the first city Cain."
                        Cowley.

O for a lodge in some vast wilderness,
Some boundless contiguity of shade,
Where rumor of oppression and deceit,
Of unsuccessful or successful war,
Might never reach me more.

Book ii. The Timepiece.

Mountains interposed
Make enemies of nations, who had else,
Like kindred drops, been mingled into one.

England with all thy faults, I love thee still.

Praise enough
To fill the ambition of a private man,
That Chatham's language was his mother tongue.

There is a pleasure in poetic pains
Which only poets know.

Variety 's the very spice of life,
That gives it all its flavor.

Domestic Happiness, thou only bliss
Of Paradise that hast survived the fall!

How various his employments whom the world
Calls idle; and who justly in return
Esteems that busy world an idler too!

Book iii. The Garden.

And while the bubbling and loud hissing urn
Throws up a steamy column, and the cups,
That cheer but not inebriate, wait on each,
So let us welcome peaceful evening in.
'T is pleasant, through the loopholes of retreat,
To peep at such a world; to see the stir
Of the great Babel, and not feel the crowd.

Book iv. Winter Evening.

He is the freeman whom the truth makes free.

Book v. Winter Morning Walk.

There is in souls a sympathy with sounds;
And as the mind is pitched, the ear is pleased
With melting airs, or martial, brisk, or grave;
Some chord in unison with what we hear
Is touched within us, and the heart replies.

> Here the heart
> May give a useful lesson to the head,
> And Learning wiser grow without his books.
>> Book vi. *Winter Walk at Noon.*

Tirocinium

> Shine by the side of every path we tread
> With such a lustre, he that runs may read.

Retirement

> Built God a church, and laughed His word to scorn.

> How sweet, how passing sweet is solitude!
> But grant me still a friend in my retreat,
> Whom I may whisper, Solitude is sweet.

Conversation

> A fool must now and then be right, by chance.

John Gilpin

> That, though on pleasure she was bent,
> She had a frugal mind.

> To dash through thick and thin.

> A hat not much the worse for wear.

Lines to his Mother's Picture

> O that those lips had language! Life has passed
> With me but roughly since I heard thee last.

Walking with God

> What peaceful hours I once enjoyed!
> How sweet their memory still!
> But they have left an aching void,
> The world can never fill.

VERSES

Supposed to be Written by Alexander Selkirk

> I am monarch of all I survey,
> My right there is none to dispute.

> O Solitude! where are the charms
> That sages have seen in thy face?

But the sound of the church-going bell
　Those valleys and rocks never heard,
Never sighed at the sound of a knell,
　Or smiled when a Sabbath appeared.

How fleet is a glance of the mind!
　Compared with the speed of its flight,
The tempest itself lags behind,
　And the swift-winged arrows of light.

W. J. MICKLE — (1734-1788)

The Mariner's Wife

His very foot has music in 't
　As he comes up the stairs.

JOHN LANGHORNE — (1735-1779)

The Country Justice

Bent o'er her babe, her eye dissolved in dew;
The big drops, mingling with the milk he drew,
Gave the sad presage of his future years,
The child of misery, baptized in tears.   **Part i.**

DR. WALCOTT — (1738-1819)

Peter Pindar's Expostulatory Odes to a great Duke and
a little Lord. Ode XV.

Care to our coffin adds a nail, no doubt,
And every grin, so merry, draws one out.

MRS. BARBAULD — (1743-1825)

Warrington Academy

Man is the noblest growth our realms supply,
And souls are ripened in our northern sky.

SIR WILLIAM JONES — (1746-1794)

A Persian Song of Hafiz

Go boldly forth, my simple lay,

Whose accents flow with artless ease,
Like orient pearls at random strung.

Ode in Imitation of Alcoeus

What constitutes a state?

.   .   .   .   .

Men who their duties know,
But know their rights, and, knowing, dare maintain.

.   .   .   .   .

And sovereign law, that state's collected will,
O'er thrones and globes elate,
Sits empress, crowning good, repressing ill.
Seven hours to law, to soothing slumber seven,
Ten to the world allot, and all to heaven.*

CAPTAIN CHARLES MORRIS — (-1832)

Billy Pitt and the Farmer

Solid men of Boston, make no long orations;
Solid men of Boston, drink no deep potations.

JOHN TRUMBULL — (1750-1831)

But optics sharp it needs, I ween,
To see what is not to be seen.
McFingal. Canto i. Line 67.

No man e'er felt the halter draw,
With good opinion of the law.
Canto iii. Line 489.

RICHARD BRINSLEY SHERIDAN — (1751-1816)

As headstrong as an allegory on the banks of the Nile.
The Rivals. Act v. Sc. 3.

My valor is certainly going! it is sneaking off! I feel
it oozing out as it were at the palm of my hands.
The Critic. Act ii. Sc. 1.

---

* "Six hours in sleep, in law's grave study six,
Four spend in prayer, the rest on nature fix."
Sir Edward Coke.

Where they *do* agree, their unanimity is wonderful.
                                        Act ii. Sc. 2.

You shall see a beautiful quarto page, where a neat rivulet of text shall meander through a meadow of margin.
                            School for Scandal. Act i. Sc. 1.

Here's to the maiden of bashful fifteen;
  Here 's to the widow of fifty;
Here 's to the flaunting, extravagant quean,
  And here's to the housewife that's thrifty.
    Let the toast pass;
    Drink to the lass;
I'll warrant she'll prove an excuse for the glass.
                                        Act iii. Sc. 3.

  I ne'er could any lustre see
  In eyes that would not look on me;
  I ne'er saw nectar on a lip
  But where my own did hope to sip.
                            The Duenna. Act i. Sc. 2,

Speech in Reply to Mr. Dundas

The Right Honorable gentleman is indebted to his memory for his jests and to his imagination for his facts.

GEORGE CRABBE — (1754-1832)

Parish Register

Oh! rather give me commentators plain,
Who with no deep researches vex the brain,
Who from the dark and doubtful love to run,
And hold their glimmering taper to the sun.

The Borough Schools

Books cannot always please, however good;
Minds are not ever craving for their food.

The Borough Players

In this fool's paradise he drank delight.

The Birth of Flattery

In idle wishes fools supinely stay;
Be there a will, — then wisdom finds a way.

ROBERT BURNS — (1759-1796)

Tam O'Shanter

Where sits our sulky, sullen dame,
Gatherin' her brows like gatherin' storm,
Nursin' her wrath to keep it warm.

Kings may be blest, but Tam was glorious,
O'er a' the ills o' life victorious.

But pleasures are like poppies spread,
You seize the flower, its bloom is shed;
Or like the snow falls in the river,
A moment white, then melts for ever.

As Tammie gloured, amazed and curious,
The mirth and fun grew fast and furious.

To a Mouse

The best laid schemes o' mice an' men
            Gang aft a-gley;
An' lea'e us naught but grief and pain
            For promised joy.

Scots wha hae

Let us do, or die!

Address to the Unco Guid

Then gently scan your brother man,
    Still gentler, sister woman;
Though they may gang a kennin' wrang,
    To step aside is human.

On Captain Grose's Peregrinations through Scotland

If there's a hole in a' your coats,
            I rede you tent it;

A chiel 's amang you takin' notes,
An', faith, he 'll prent it.

To a Louse

O wad some power the giftie gie us,
To see oursel's as others see us!
It wad frae monie a blunder free us,
An' foolish notion.

Epistle to a Young Friend

The fear o' hell 's a hangman's whip
To haud the wretch in order;
But where ye feel your honor grip,
Let that aye be your border.

The Twa Dogs

His locked, lettered, braw brass collar
Shawed him the gentleman and scholar.

Epistle to James Smith

O Life! how pleasant in thy morning,
Young Fancy's rays the hills adorning!
Cold, pausing Caution's lesson scorning,
We frisk away,
Like schoolboys at th' expected warning,

To joy and play.

Despondency

O life! thou art a galling load,
Along a rough, a weary road,
To wretches such as I!

Auld Lang Syne

Should auld acquaintance be forgot,
And never brought to min'?
Should auld acquaintance be forgot,
And days o' lang syne?

Green grow the Rashes

Her 'prentice han' she tried on man,
And then she made the lasses, O!

Man was made to Mourn

Man's inhumanity to man
Makes countless thousands mourn.

Death and Dr. Hornbook

Some wee short hour ayont the twal.

Is there for honest Poverty

The *rank* is but the guinea's *stamp*,
   The man 's the gowd for a' that.

A prince can mak' a belted knight,
   A marquis, duke, and a' that;
But an honest man 's aboon his might,
   Guid faith, he maunna fa' that.

The Cotter's Saturday Night

He wales a portion with judicious care;
And "Let us worship God!" he says, with solemn air.

THOMAS MOSS — (-1808)

The Beggar

Pity the sorrows of a poor old man,
   Whose trembling limbs have borne him to your door,
Whose days are dwindled to the shortest span;
   Oh! give relief, and Heaven will bless your store.

GEORGE COLMAN — (1762-1836)

BROAD GRINS

The Maid of the Moor
And what 's impossible can't be,

And never, never comes to pass.

Three stories high, long, dull, and old,
As great lord's stories often are.

Lodgings for Single Gentlemen

But when ill indeed,
E'en dismissing the doctor don't always succeed.

The Poor Gentleman

Thank you, good sir, I owe you one.   Act i. Sc. 2.

Prologue to the Heir at Law

On their own merits modest men are dumb.

THOMAS MORTON — (1764-1836)

What will Mrs. Grundy say?
                    Speed the Plough. Act i. Sc. 1.

GEORGE CANNING — (1770-1827)

POETRY OF THE ANTI-JACOBIN

The Needy Knife-Grinder

Story! God bless you, I have none to tell, sir!

I give thee sixpence! I will see thee d——d first.

The Loves of the Triangles

So down thy hill, romantic Ashbourne, glides
The Derby dilly, carrying three insides.   Line 178.

WILLIAM WORDSWORTH — (1770-1850)

Guilt and Sorrow

And homeless near a thousand homes I stood,
And near a thousand tables pined and wanted food.

My Heart Leaps Up

The Child is father of the Man.

Lucy Gray

The sweetest thing that ever grew
Beside a human door.   St. 2.

We are Seven

A simple Child,
That lightly draws its breath,
And feels its life in every limb,
What should it know of death?

The Pet Lamb

Drink, pretty creature, drink.

The Brothers

Until a man might travel twelve stout miles,
Or reap an acre of his neighbor's corn.

Stanzas written in Thomson

A noticeable man, with large gray eyes.

Lucy

She dwelt among the untrodden ways
   Beside the springs of Dove,
A maid whom there were none to praise,
   And very few to love:

A violet by a mossy stone
   Half hidden from the eye!
Fair as a star, when only one
   Is shining in the sky.

She lived unknown, and few could know
   When Lucy ceased to be;
But she is in her grave, and oh!
   The difference to me!

The Solitary Reaper

Some natural sorrow, loss, or pain,
That has been, and may be again.

.　　　.　　　.　　　.　　　　　.

The music in my heart I bore,
Long after it was heard no more.

Rob Roy's Grave

Because the good old rule
Sufficeth them, the simple plan,
That they should take who have the power,
And they should keep who can.　　　　St. 9.

Yarrow Unvisited

The swan on still St. Mary's Lake

Float double, swan and shadow!

Sonnets to National Independence and Liberty

Men are we, and must grieve when even the Shade
Of that which once was great is passed away.
　　　　　　　　　　　　　　　　　Part i. vi.
Thy soul was like a Star, and dwelt apart.　　　**Part i. xiv.**
We must be free or die, who speak the tongue
That Shakespeare spake; the faith and morals hold
Which Milton held.　　　　　　　　　　　**Part i. xvi.**

Nutting

One of those heavenly days that cannot die.

She was a Phantom of Delight

A Creature not too bright or good
For human nature's daily food,
For transient sorrows, simple wiles;
Praise, blame, love, kisses, tears, and smiles.

.　　　.　　　.　　　.　　　　.

A perfect woman, nobly planned,
To warn, to comfort, and command.

I Wandered Lonely

That inward eye
Which is the bliss of solitude.

Ruth

A Youth to whom was given
So much of earth, so much of heaven.

Resolution and Independence

I thought of Chatterton, the marvellous Boy,
The sleepless soul that perished in his pride;
Of him who walked in glory and in joy,
Following his plough, along the mountain-side.

Part i. St. 7.

Hart-Leap Well

"A jolly place," said he, "in times of old!
But something ails it now: the spot is cursed."

Never to blend our pleasure or our pride
With sorrow of the meanest thing that feels.

Part ii.

Tintern Abbey

Sensations sweet,
Felt in the blood, and felt along the heart.
That best portion of a good man's life,
His little, nameless, unremembered acts
Of kindness and of love.

.   .   .   .   .

That blessed mood,
In which the burden of the mystery,
In which the heavy and the weary weight
Of all this unintelligible world,
Is lightened.

The fretful stir
Unprofitable, and the fever of the world,
Have hung upon the beatings of my heart.

The sounding cataract
Haunted me like a passion; the tall rock,
The mountain, and the deep and gloomy wood,
Their colors and their forms, were then to me
An appetite; a feeling and a love,
That had no need of a remoter charm
By thoughts supplied, nor any interest
Unborrowed from the eye.

But hearing oftentimes
The still, sad music of humanity.

To a Skylark

Type of the wise who soar, but never roam;
True to the kindred points of Heaven and Home.

Peter Bell

There's something in a flying horse,
There's something in a huge balloon.
Prologue. St. 1.

The common growth of Mother Earth
Suffices me, — her tears, her mirth,
Her humblest mirth and tears.
Prologue. St. 27.

A primrose by a river's brim
A yellow primrose was to him,
And it was nothing more.
Part i. St. 12.

The soft blue sky did never melt
Into his heart; he never felt
The witchery of the soft blue sky!
Part i. St. 15.

As if the man had fixed his face,
In many a solitary place,
Against the wind and open sky!   Part i. St. 26.

Miscellaneous Sonnets

The holy time is quiet as a Nun
Breathless with adoration.   Part i. xxx.

The world is too much with us; late and soon,
Getting and spending, we lay waste our powers.
Part i. xxxiii.

'T is hers to pluck the amaranthine flower
Of Faith, and round the Sufferer's temples bind
Wreaths that endure affliction's heaviest shower,
And do not shrink from sorrow's keenest wind.

Part i. xxxv

Dear God! the very houses seem asleep;
And all that mighty heart is lying still!

Part ii. xxxvi.

Ecclesiastical Sonnets

The feather, whence the pen
Was shaped that traced the lives of these good men,
Dropped from an Angel's wing.

.   .   .   .   .

Meek Walton's heavenly memory.

Part iii. v. *Walton's Book of Lives.*

The Tables Turned

Up! up! my Friend, and quit your books,
Or surely you 'll grow double:
Up! up! my Friend, and clear your looks;
Why all this toil and trouble?

.   .   .   .   .

One impulse from a vernal wood
May teach you more of man,
Of moral evil and of good,
Than all the sages can.

A Poet's Epitaph

One that would peep and botanize
Upon his mother's grave.

St. 5.

Personal Talk

The gentle Lady married to the Moor,
And heavenly Una with her milk-white Lamb.

St. 3.

The Small Celandine

[From Poems referring to the Period of Old Age.]
To be a Prodigal's Favorite, — then, worse truth,

A Miser's Pensioner, — behold our lot!

*Elegiac Stanzas suggested by a Picture of Peele Castle
in a Storm.   St. 4.*

The light that never was, on sea or land,
The consecration, and the Poet's dream.

Intimations of Inmortality.   St. 5.

Our birth is but a sleep and a forgetting.

.   .   .   .   .

But trailing clouds of glory, do we come
    From God, who is our home:
Heaven lies about us in our infancy!
To me the meanest flower that blows can give
Thoughts that do often lie too deep for tears.   St. xi.

THE EXCURSION

The vision and the faculty divine.   Book i.

The imperfect offices of prayer and praise.

The good die first,
And they whose hearts are dry as summer dust
Burn to the socket.
With battlements, that on their restless fronts
Bore stars.   Book ii.
Wrongs unredressed, or insults unavenged.   Book iii.
            Monastic brotherhood, upon rock
Aerial.   Book iv.
                    I have seen
A curious child, who dwelt upon a tract
Of inland ground, applying to his ear
The convolutions of a smooth-lipped shell.
To which, in silence hushed, his very soul
Listened intensely; and his countenance soon
Brightened with joy; for from within were heard
Murmurings, whereby the monitor expressed
Mysterious union with its native sea.

            One in whom persuasion and belief
Had ripened into faith, and faith become
A passionate intuition.   Book iv.
Spires whose silent fingers point to heaven.   Book vi.
Wisdom married to immortal verse.   Book vii.

The primal duties shine aloft, like stars;
The charities, that soothe, and heal, and bless,
Are scattered at the feet of Man, like flowers.　　Book ix.

HON. WILLIAM ROBERT SPENCER — (1770-1834)

Lines to Lady A. Hamilton

Too late I stayed, — forgive the crime;
　Unheeded flew the hours.
How noiseless falls the foot of time,
　That only treads on flowers!

DR. GEORGE SEWELL — (　-1726)

When all the blandishments of life are gone,
The coward sneaks to death, the brave live on.

SAMUEL TAYLOR COLERIDGE — (1772-1834)

The Ancient Mariner

And listens like a three years' child.　　Part i.
We were the first that ever burst
Into that silent sea.
As idle as a painted ship
Upon a painted ocean.
Water, water, everywhere,
Nor any drop to drink.　　Part ii.
Alone, alone, all, all alone,
Alone on a wide, wide sea.　　Part iv.
A noise like of a hidden brook
In the leafy month of June.　　Part v.
He prayeth well, who loveth well
Both man and bird and beast.
He prayeth best, who loveth best
All things, both great and small.
A sadder and a wiser man,
He rose the morrow morn.　　Part vii.

Christabel

Alas! they had been friends in youth;
But whispering tongues can poison truth;
And constancy lives in realms above.

The Devil's Thoughts

And the Devil did grin, for his darling sin,
  Is pride that apes humility.

Love

All thoughts, all passions, all delights,
Whatever stirs this mortal frame,
All are but ministers of Love,
And feel his sacred flame.

Reflections on having left a Place of Retirement.

Blest hour! it was a luxury — to be!

Hymn in the Vale of Chamouni

Hast thou a charm to stay the morning star
In his steep course?
Risest from forth thy silent sea of pines.
Motionless torrents! silent cataracts!
Earth, with her thousand voices, praises God.

The Three Graves

A mother is a mother still,
  The holiest thing alive.

The Visit of the Gods

Never, believe me,
Appear the Immortals,
Never alone.

The Knight's Tomb

The Knight's bones are dust,
And his good sword rust;
His soul is with the saints, I trust.

On Taking Leave of ———. 1817

To know, to esteem, to love — and then to part,
Makes up life's tale to many a feeling heart!

Cologne

The river Rhine, it is well known,
Doth wash your city of Cologne;

But tell me, nymphs! what power divine
Shall henceforth wash the river Rhine?   Part ii.

Wallenstein

The intelligible forms of ancient poets,
The fair humanities of old religion,
The power, the beauty, and the majesty,
That had their haunts in dale, or piny mountain,
Or forest by slow stream, or pebbly spring,
Or chasms and watery depths; all these have vanished;
They live no longer in the faith of reason.
                              Part i. Act ii. Sc. 4.

The Death of Wallenstein

Clothing the palpable and familiar
With golden exhalations of the dawn.   Act v. Sc. 1.
                Often do the spirits
Of great events stride on before the events,
And in to-day already walks to-morrow.   Act v. Sc. 1.

ROBERT SOUTHEY — (1774-1843)

They sin who tell us love can die.
With life all other passions fly,
    All others are but vanity.   *Curse of Kehama.* Canto x.

CHARLES LAMB — (1775-1834)

Old Familiar Faces

I have had playmates, I have had companions,
In my days of childhood, in my joyful school-days;
All, all are gone, the old familiar faces.

Detached Thoughts on Books

Books which are no books.

THOMAS CAMPBELL — (1777-1844)

PLEASURES OF HOPE

'T is distance lends enchantment to the view,
And robes the mountain in its azure hue.   Part i. Line 7.
O Heaven! he cried, my bleeding country save.   Line 359.
Hope for a season bade the world farewell,
And Freedom shrieked as Kosciusko fell!

O'er Prague's proud arch the fires of ruin glow,
His blood-dyed waters murmuring far below.   Line 381.
Who hath not owned, with rapture-smitten frame,
The power of grave, the magic of a name?   Part ii. Line 5.
Without the smile from partial beauty won,
O what were man? — a world without a sun.   Line 23.
The world was sad! — the garden was a wild!
And man, the hermit, sighed — till woman smiled. Line 37.
While Memory watches o'er the sad review
Of joys that faded like the morning dew.   Line 45.
There shall he love, when genial morn appears,
Like pensive Beauty smiling in her tears.   Line 95.
That gems the starry girdle of the year.   Line 194.
Melt, and dispel, ye spectre-doubts, that roll
Cimmerian darkness o'er the parting soul!   Line 263.
O star-eyed Science! hast thou wandered there,
To waft us home the message of despair?   Line 325.

O'Conner's Child

Another's sword has laid him low,
    Another's and another's;
And every hand that dealt the blow,
    Ah me! it was a brother's!

Lochiel's Warning

'T is the sunset of life gives me mystical lore,
And coming events cast their shadows before.

Ye Mariners of England

Ye mariners of England!
    That guard our native seas,
Whose flag has braved, a thousand years,
    The battle and the breeze.

Britannia needs no bulwarks,
    No towers along the steep;
Her march is o'er the mountain waves,
    Her home is on the deep.

The Soldier's Dream

In life's morning march, when my bosom was young.

But sorrow returned with the dawning of morn,
And the voice in my dreaming ear melted away.

Hohenlinden

The combat deepens. On, ye brave,
Who rush to glory, or the grave!

Gertrude of Wyoming

O love! in such a wilderness as this.   Part iii. St. 1.

WALTER SCOTT — (1771-1832)

THE LAY OF THE LAST MINSTREL

If thou wouldst view fair Melrose aright,
Go visit it by the pale moonlight.   Canto ii. St. 1.
I was not always a man of woe.   Canto ii. St. 12.
I cannot tell how the truth may be;
I say the tale as 't was said to me.   Canto ii. St. 22.
Love rules the court, the camp, the grove,
And men below and saints above;
For love is heaven, and heaven is love.   Canto iii. St. 2.
Call it not vain; — they do not err,
Who say, that, when the poet dies,
Mute Nature mourns her worshipper,
And celebrates his obsequies.   Canto v. St. 1.
True love 's the gift which God has given
To man alone beneath the heaven.

.   .   .   .   .

It is the secret sympathy,
The silver link, the silken tie,
Which heart to heart, and mind to mind,
In body and in soul can bind.   Canto v. St. 13.
Breathes there the man, with soul so dead,
Who never to himself hath said,
This is my own, my native land!
Whose heart hath ne'er within him burned,
As home his footsteps he hath turned
From wandering on a foreign strand?

.   .   .   .   .

Unwept, unhonored, and unsung.   Canto vi. St. 1.

O Caledonia! stern and wild,
Meet nurse for a poetic child!
Land of brown heath and shaggy wood;
Land of the mountain and the flood.   Canto vi. St. 2.

Marmion

'T is an old tale, and often told.   Canto ii. St. 27.
With a smile on her lips and a tear in her eye.
                                        Canto v. St. 12.

And dar'st thou then

To beard the lion in his den?   Canto vi. St. 14.
  O woman! in our hours of ease,
  Uncertain, coy, and hard to please,
  And variable as the shade
  By the light quivering aspen made,
  When pain and anguish wring the brow,
  A ministering angel thou!   Canto vi. St. 30.
  Charge, Chester, charge! On, Stanley, on!
  Were the last words of Marmion.   Canto vi. St. 32.

  To all, to each, a fair good night,
And pleasing dreams, and slumbers light.
                                    Canto vi. Last Lines.

The Lady of the Lake

And ne'er did Grecian chisel trace
A nymph, a naiad, or a grace,
Of finer form or lovelier face.

         .   .   .   .   .

A foot more light, a step more true,
Ne'er from the heath-flower dashed the dew.
                                        Canto i. St. 18.

On his bold visage middle age
Had slightly pressed its signet sage.   Canto i. St. 21.
Some feelings are to mortals given
With less of earth in them than heaven.   Canto ii. St .22.
The rose is fairest when 't is budding new,
And hope is brightest when it dawns from fears.
                                        Canto iv. St. 1.
Art thou a friend to Roderick?   Canto iv. St. 30.
Come one, come all! this rock shall fly
From its firm base as soon as I.

         .   .   .   .   .

And the stern joy which warriors feel
In foemen worthy of their steel.   Canto v. St. 10.

The Lord of the Isles

  O many a shaft, at random sent,

Finds mark, the archer little meant!
And many a word at random spoken
May soothe, or wound, a heart that 's broken!

Old Mortality

Sound, sound the clarion, fill the fife!
    To all the sensual world proclaim,
One crowded hour of glorious life
    Is worth an age without a name. Vol. ii. Chapter xxi.

Rob Roy

O for the voice of that wild horn
On Fontarabian echoes borne.   Vol. i. Chapter ii.

The Monastery

Within that awful volume lies
The mystery of mysteries!   Vol. i. Chapter ii.

THOMAS MOORE — (1780-1852)

Lalla Rookh. The Fire-Worshippers

O, ever thus from childhood's hour
    I 've seen my fondest hopes decay;
I never loved a tree or flower,
    But 't was the first to fade away.

The Light of the Harem

Alas! how light a cause may move
Dissension between hearts that love!
Hearts that the world in vain had tried,
And sorrow but more closely tied;
That stood the storm when waves were rough,
Yet in a sunny hour fall off,
Like ships that have gone down at sea,
When heaven was all tranquillity.

All that 's bright must fade

All that 's bright must fade, —
    The brightest still the fleetest;
All that 's sweet was made
    But to be lost when sweetest.

Farewell! But whenever you welcome the hour

You may break, you may shatter the vase, if you will,
But the scent of the roses will hang round it still.

REGINALD HEBER — (1783-1826)

Christmas Hymn

Brightest and best of the sons of the morning!
Dawn on our darkness, and lend us thine aid.

Missionary Hymn

From Greenland's icy mountains,
From India's coral strand,
Where Afric's sunny fountains
Roll down their golden sand.

Palestine

No hammers fell, no ponderous axes rung;
Like some tall palm, the mystic fabric sprung.
Majestic silence!

JONATHAN M. SEWALL

Written for the Bow Street Theatre, Portsmouth, N.H., 1778

No pent-up Utica contracts your powers,
But the whole boundless continent is yours.

Epilogue to Cato.

SAMUEL WOODWORTH — (1785-1842)

The old oaken bucket, the iron-bound bucket,
The moss-covered bucket, which hung in the well.

LORD BYRON — (1788-1821)

Childe Harold

Maidens, like moths, are ever caught by glare,
And Mammon wins his way where Seraphs might despair.

Canto i. St. 9.

.   .   .   .   .

A school-boy's tale, the wonder of an hour!
Dim with the mist of years, gray flits the shade of power.

Canto ii. St. 2.

The dome of Thought, the palace of the soul.   Stanza 6.
Ah! happy years! once more who would not be a boy?
                                              Stanza 23.
Fair Greece! sad relic of departed worth!
Immortal, though no more; though fallen, great! Stanza 73.
Hereditary bondsmen! know ye not,
Who would be free, themselves must strike the blow?
                                              Stanza 76.
Where'er we tread, 't is haunted, holy ground.

     .   .   .   .

Age shakes Athena's towers, but spares gray Marathon.
                                              Stanza 88.
Ada! sole daughter of my house and heart.   Canto iii. St. 1.
There was a sound of revelry by night.

     .   .   .   .   .

And all went merry as a marriage-bell.   Stanza 21.
Battle's magnificently stern array!   Stanza 28.
The castled crag of Drachenfels
Frowns o'er the wide and winding Rhine.   Stanza 55.
The sky is changed! and such a change! O night,
And storm, and darkness! ye are wondrous strong,
Yet lovely in your strength, as is the light
Of a dark eye in woman.   Stanza 92.
I have not loved the world, nor the world me. Stanza 113.
I stood in Venice, on the Bridge of Sighs.   Canto iv. St. 1.
The cold — the changed — perchance the deal anew,
The mourned — the loved — the lost — too many! yet how
    few!   Stanza 24.
                       Fills
The air around with beauty.   Stanza 49.
The hell of waters! where they howl and hiss. Stanza 69.
The Niobe of nations! there she stands.   Stanza 79.
                       Man!
Thou pendulum betwixt a smile and tear.   Stanza 109.
The nympholepsy of some fond despair.   Stanza 115.
While stands the Coliseum, Rome shall stand;
When falls the Coliseum, Rome shall fall;
And when Rome falls, the world.*   Stanza 145.
O that the desert were my dwelling-place,
With one fair spirit for my minister,

---

   * The exclamation of the pilgrims in the eighth century, as recorded by the venerable Bede.

That I might all forget the human race,
And, hating no one, love but only her!   Stanza 177.
There is a pleasure in the pathless woods,
There is a rapture on the lonely shore,
There is society where none intrudes
By the deep Sea, and music in its roar.

.   .   .   .   .

I love not Man the less, but Nature more.   Stanza 178.
Without a grave, unknelled, uncoffined, and unknown.
                                                  Stanza 179.
          And what is writ, is writ.
Would it were worthier!   Stanza 185.

Memoranda from his Life

I awoke one morning and found myself famous.

The Giaour

Before decay's effacing fingers
Have swept the lines where beauty lingers.   Line 72.
So coldly sweet, so deadly fair,
We start, for soul is wanting there.   Line 92.
Shrine of the mighty! can it be
That this is all remains of thee?   Line 106.
For freedom's battle, once begun,
Bequeathed by bleeding sire to son,
Though baffled oft, is ever won.   Line 123.
And lovelier things have mercy shown
To every failing but their own;
And every woe a tear can claim,
Except an erring sister's shame.   Line 418.

Parasina

It is the hour when from the boughs
     The nightingale's high note is heard;
It is the hour when lovers' vows
     Seem sweet in every whispered word.   St. 1.

The Bride of Abydos

Know ye the land where the cypress and myrtle.
                                        Canto i. St. 1.
The light of love, the purity of grace,
The mind, the music breathing from her face,
The heart whose softness harmonized the whole,

And oh! that eye was in itself a soul!   Stanza 6.
Be thou the rainbow to the storms of life!
The evening beam that smiles the clouds away,
And tints to-morrow with prophetic ray!

    .   .   .   .   .

He makes a solitude, and calls it — peace.*   Canto ii. St. 20.

Darkness

I had a dream which was not all a dream.

Lara

Lord of himself, — that heritage of woe!   Canto i. St. 2.

The Corsair

O'er the glad waters of the dark blue sea,
Our thoughts as boundless, and our souls as free,
Far as the breeze can bear, the billows foam,
Survey our empire, and behold our home.   Canto i. St. 1.
She walks the waters like a thing of life,
And seems to dare the elements to strife.   Stanza 3.
The power of Thought, — the magic of the Mind.

    .   .   .   .

The many still must labor for the one!   Stanza 8.
There was a laughing devil in his sneer.
Hope withering fled, and Mercy sighed Farewell!   Stanza 9.
                Farewell!
For in that word, — that fatal word, — howe'er
We promise — hope — believe, — there breathes despair.
                    Stanza 15.
No words suffice the secret soul to show,
For truth denies all eloquence to woe.   Canto iii. St. 22.
He left a corsair's name to other times,
Linked with one virtue, and a thousand crimes.   Stanza 24.

Beppo

For most men (till by losing rendered sager)
Will back their own opinions by a wager.   Stanza 27.
Heart on her lips, and soul within her eyes,
Soft as her clime, and sunny as her skies.   Stanza 45.
O Mirth and Innocence! O Milk and Water!

---

* "Solitudinem faciunt, — pacem appellant."
                    Tacitus, Agricola, cap. 30.

Ye happy mixtures of more happy days!   Stanza 80.

The Dream

And both were young, and one was beautiful.

And to his eye
There was but one beloved face on earth,
And that was shining on him.

A change came o'er the spirit of my dream.

And they were canopied by the blue sky,
So cloudless, clear, and purely beautiful,
That God alone was to be seen in Heaven.

The Waltz

Hand promiscuously applied,
Round the slight waist, or down the glowing side.

English Bards

'T is pleasant, sure, to see one's name in print;
A book 's a book, although there 's nothing in t'.

As soon
Seek roses in December, — ice in June.
Hope constancy in wind, or corn in chaff.

.   .   .   .   .

Believe a woman, or an epitaph,
Or any other thing that 's false, before
You trust in critics.

Perverts the Prophets, and purloins the Psalms.

O Amos Cottle! Phoebus! what a name!

Monody on the Death of Sheridan

When all of Genius which can perish dies.

Folly loves the martyrdom of Fame.

Who track the steps of Glory to the grave.

Sighing that Nature formed but one such man,
And broke the die in moulding Sheridan.

Don Juan

But, O ye lords of ladies intellectual!

Inform us truly, have they not henpecked you all?
Canto i. St. 22.
Whispering I will ne'er consent, consented. Canto i. St. 117.
Society is now one polished horde,
Formed of two mighty tribes, the *Bores* and *Bored*.
Canto xiii. St. 95.
The Devil hath not, in all his quiver's choice,
An arrow for the heart like a sweet voice. Canto xv. St. 13.

Hebrew Melodies

She walks in beauty, like the night
  Of cloudless climes and starry skies;
And all that 's best of dark and bright
  Meet in her aspect and her eyes;
Thus mellowed to that tender light
  Which Heaven to gaudy day denies.

CHARLES WOLFE — (1791-1823)

The Burial of Sir John Moore

Not a drum was heard, not a funeral note.

.   .   .   .   .

We carved not a line, and we raised not a stone,
But we left him alone with his glory!

JOSEPH RODMAN DRAKE — (1795-1820)

The American Flag

When Freedom from her mountain height
  Unfurled her standard to the air,
She tore the azure robe of night,
  And set the stars of glory there.

JOHN KEATS — (1796-1820)

Endymion

A thing of beauty is a joy for ever.   Line 1.

St. Agnes' Eve

Music's golden tongue
Flattered to tears this aged man and poor.   Stanza 27.

ROBERT POLLOK — (1789-1827)

The Course of Time

He was a man
Who stole the livery of the court of Heaven
To serve the Devil in.   Book viii. Line 616.

THOMAS HOOD — (1798-1845)

The Death-Bed

We watched her breathing through the night,
  Her breathing soft and low.
As in her breast the wave of life
  Kept heaving to and fro.

    .   .   .   .   .

Our very hopes belied our fears,
  Our fears our hopes belied;
We thought her dying when she slept,
  And sleeping when she died.

The Bridge of Sighs

One more Unfortunate
Weary of breath,
Rashly importunate,
Gone to her death.

Take her up tenderly,
Lift her with care;
Fashioned so slenderly,
Young, and so fair!

SAMUEL ROGERS

Human Life

A guardian-angel o'er his life presiding,
Doubling his pleasures, and his cares dividing.

    .   .   .   .   .

The soul of music slumbers in the shell,
Till waked and kindled by the master's spell;
And feeling hearts — touch them but rightly — pour
A thousand melodies unheard before!

    .   .   .   .   .

Then, never less alone than when alone,
Those that he loved so long and sees no more,
Loved and still loves, — not dead, but gone before, —
He gathers round him.

A Wish

Mine be a cot beside the hill;
  A beehive's hum shall soothe my ear;
A willowy brook, that turns a mill,
  With many a fall, shall linger near.

RICHARD MONCKTON MILNES

Tragedy of the Lac de Gaube

But on and up, where Nature's heart
  Beats strong amid the hills.   Stanza 2.

The Men of Old

Great thoughts, great feelings, came to them,
  Like instincts, unawares.

A man's best things are nearest him,
  Lie close about his feet.

BRYAN W. PROCTOR

The Sea

The sea! the sea! the open sea!
The blue, the fresh, the ever free!

I never was on the dull, tame shore,
But I loved the great sea more and more.

ALFRED TENNYSON

Locksley Hall

He will hold thee, when his passion shall have spent its
    novel force,
Something better than his dog, a little dearer than his horse.

   .   .   .   .   .

I will take some savage woman, she shall rear my dusky
    race.

   .   .   .   .   .

Better fifty years of Europe than a cycle of Cathay.

In Memoriam

'T is better to have loved and lost.
Than never to have loved at all.   xxvii.

Fatima

O Love, O fire! once he drew
With one long kiss my whole soul through
My lips, as sunlight drinketh dew.   St. 3.

The Princess

Tears, idle tears, I know not what they mean,
Tears from the depth of some divine despair
Rise in the heart, and gather to the eyes,
In looking on the happy Autumn fields,
And thinking of the days that are no more.
    Dear as remembered kisses after death,
And sweet as those by hopeless fancy feigned
On lips that are for others; deep as love,
Deep as first love, and wild with all regret;
O Death in Life, the days that are no more.   Canto iv.
          Sweet is every sound,
Sweeter thy voice, but every sound is sweet;
Myriads of rivulets hurrying through the lawn,
The moan of doves in immemorial elms,
And murmuring of innumerable bees.

                    Happy he
With such a mother! faith in womankind
Beats with his blood, and trust in all things high
Comes easy to him, and though he trip and fall,
He shall not blind his soul with clay.   Canto 7.

Lady Clara Vere de Vere

From yon blue heaven above us bent,
The grand old gardener and his wife
    Smile at the claims of long descent.

HEKIRY TAYLOR

Philip Van Artevelde

The world knows nothing of its greatest men.
                    Part i. Act i. Sc. 5.

EDWARD BULWER LYTTON

Beneath the rule of men entirely great
The pen is mightier than the sword. *Richelieu*. Act ii. Sc. 2.

PHILIP JAMES BAILEY

Festus

We live in deeds, not years; in thoughts, not breaths;
In feelings, not in figures on a dial.
We should count time by heart-throbs. He most lives
Who thinks most, feels the noblest, acts the best.

THOMAS K. HERVEY

The Devil's Progress

The tomb of him who would have made
    The world too glad and free.

.   .   .   .   .

He stood beside a cottage lone,
    And listened to a lute,
One summer's eve, when the breeze was gone,
    And the nightingale was mute!

.   .   .   .   .

Like ships, that sailed for sunny isles,
    But never came to shore!

JAMES ALDRICH

A Death-Bed

Her suffering ended with the day,

    Yet lived she at its close,
And breathed the long, long night away,
    In statue-like repose!

But when the sun, in all his state,
    Illumed the eastern skies,
She passed through Glory's morning gate,
    And walked in Paradise.

WILLIAM CULLEN BRYANT

Thanatopsis

To him who in the love of Nature holds

Communion with her visible forms, she speaks
A various language.

. . . .

Go forth, under the open sky, and list
To Nature's teachings.

.   .   . .   Sustained and soothed
By an unfaltering trust, approach thy grave,
Like one that wraps the drapery of his couch
About him, and lies down to pleasant dreams.

March

The stormy March has come at last,
    With wind and clouds and changing skies;
I hear the rushing of the blast
    That through the snowy valley flies.

Autumn Woods

But 'neath yon crimson tree,
Lover to listening maid might breathe his flame,
    Nor mark, within its roseate canopy,
        Her blush of maiden shame.

Forest Hymn

The groves were God's first temples.

The Death of the Flowers

The melancholy days are come,
    The saddest of the year,
Of wailing winds, and naked woods,
    And meadows brown and sear.

The Battle-Field

Truth crushed to earth shall rise again:
    The eternal years of God are hers;
But Error, wounded, writhes with pain,
    And dies among his worshippers.

FITZ-GREENE HALLECK

Marco Bozzaris

Strike — for your altars and your fires;

Strike — for the green graves of your sires;
  God, and your native land!

One of the few, the immortal names,
  That were not born to die.

On the Death of Joseph Rodman Drake

Green be the turf above thee,
  Friend of my better days;
None knew thee but to love thee,
  Nor named thee but to praise.

Burns

Such graves as his are pilgrim-shrines,
  Shrines to no code or creed confined, —
The Delphian vales, the Palestines,
  The Meccas of the mind.

CHARLES SPRAGUE

Curiosity

Lo, where the stage, the poor, degraded stage,
Holds its warped mirror to a gaping age.

Through life's dark road his sordid way he wends,
An incarnation of fat dividends.

Centennial Ode

Behold! in Liberty's unclouded blaze
We lift our heads, a race of other days.   Stanza 22.

To my Cigar

Yes, social friend, I love thee well,
  In learned doctors' spite;
Thy clouds all other clouds dispel,
  And lap me in delight.

HENRY W. LONGFELLOW

A Psalm of Life

Tell me not, in mournful numbers,
  "Life is but an empty dream!"
For the soul is dead that slumbers,

And things are not what they seem.

Art is long, and Time is fleeting.

Let the dead Past bury its dead!

Lives of great men all remind us
  We can make our lives sublime,
And, departing, leave behind us
  Footprints on the sands of time.
Still achieving, still pursuing,
  Learn to labor and to wait.
                    The Light of Stars

Know how sublime a thing it is
  To suffer and be strong.

                    It is not always May

For Time will teach thee soon the truth,
  There are no birds in last year's nest!

                    Maidenhood

Standing, with reluctant feet,
Where the brook and river meet,
Womanhood and childhood fleet!

                    The Goblet of Life

  O suffering, sad humanity!
  O ye afflicted ones, who lie
  Steeped to the lips in misery,
  Longing, and yet afraid to die,
    Patient, though sorely tried!

                    Resignation

There is no flock, however watched and tended,
  But one dear lamb is there!
There is no fireside, howsoe'er defended,
  But has one vacant chair.
The air is full of farewells to the dying,
  And mournings for the dead.

                    The Golden Legend

            Time has laid his hand
Upon my heart, gently, not smiting it,
But as a harper lays his open palm

Upon his harp, to deaden its vibrations.

OLIVER WENDELL HOLMES

A Metrical Essay

The freeman casting with unpurchased hand
The vote that shakes the turrets of the land.

Ay, tear her tattered ensign down!
    Long has it waved on high,
And many an eye has danced to see
    That banner in the sky.

.   .   .   .   .

Nail to the mast her holy flag,
    Set every threadbare sail,
And give her to the God of storms,
    The lightning and the gale.

Urania

Yes, child of suffering, thou mayst well be sure,
He who ordained the Sabbath loves the poor!
And, when you stick on conversation's burrs,
Don't strew your pathway with those dreadful *urs*.

The Music-Grinders

You think they are crusaders, sent
    From some infernal clime,
To pluck the eyes of Sentiment,
    And dock the tail of Rhyme,
To crack the voice of Melody,
    And break the legs of Time.

JAMES RUSSELL LOWELL

The Vision of Sir Launfal

And what is so rare as a day in June?
    Then, if ever, come perfect days;
Then Heaven tries the earth if it be in tune,
    And over it softly her warm ear lays.

The Changeling

This child is not mine as the first was,
    I cannot sing it to rest,

I cannot lift it up fatherly
  And bless it upon my breast;
Yet it lies in my little one's cradle
  And sits in my little one's chair,
And the light of the heaven she 's gone to
  Transfigures its golden hair.

WILLIAM BASSE — (1613-1648)

On Shakespeare

Renowned Spenser, lie a thought more nigh
To learned Chaucer, and rare Beaumont lie
A little nearer Spenser, to make room
For Shakespeare in your threefold, fourfold tomb.

DAVID EVERETT — (1769-1813)

Lines written for a School Declamation

You 'd scarce expect one of my age
To speak in public on the stage;
And if I chance to fall below
Demosthenes or Cicero,
Don't view me with a critic's eye,
But pass my imperfections by.
Large streams from little fountains flow,
Tall oaks from little acorns grow.

JOSEPH HOPKINSON — (1770-1842)

Hail Columbia

Hail, Columbia, happy land!
Hail, ye heroes! heaven-born band!

F. S. KEY

The Star-spangled Banner

The star-spangled banner, O long may it wave
O'er the land of the free and the home of the brave!

ALBERT G. GREENE

Old Grimes

Old Grimes is dead; that good old man,

We ne'er shall see him more:
He used to wear a long black coat,
All buttoned down before.

JOHN LOUIS UHLAND

The Passage. Translated by Mrs. Sarah Austin

Take, O boatman, thrice thy fee;
Take, — I give it willingly;
For, invisible to thee,
Spirits twain have crossed with me.

CHRISTOPHER P. CRANCH

Stanzas

Thought is deeper than all speech;
 Feeling deeper than all thought;
Souls to souls can never teach
 What unto themselves was taught.

EATON STANNARD BARRETT

Woman

Not she with trait'rous kiss her Master stung,
Not she denied him with unfaithful tongue;
She, when apostles fled, could danger brave,
Last at his cross, and earliest at his grave.

MISS FANNY STEERS

Song

The last link is broken
 That bound me to thee,
And the words thou hast spoken
 Have rendered me free.

RICHARD BAXTER — (1615-1691)

Love breathing Thanks and Praise

I preached as never sure to preach again,
And as a dying man to dying men.

ROGER L'ESTRANGE — (1616-1704)

Fables from several Authors. Fable 398

Though this may be play to you,
'T is death to us.

MISCELLANEOUS

*From Apophthegms, &c. first gathered and compiled in
Latin, by Erasmus, and now translated into English
by Nicholas Vdall. 8vo. 1542. Fol. 239.*

That same man, that rennith awaie,
Maie again fight an other daie.

*From the Musarum Deliciae, compiled by Sir John
Mennis and Dr. James Smith. 1640.*

He that fights and runs away
May live to fight another day.*

Richard Grafton. *Abridgement of the Chronicles of Englande.
1570. 8vo. "A rule to know how many dayes euery
moneth in the yeare hath."*

Thirty dayes hath Nouember,
April, June, and September,
February hath xxviii alone,
And all the rest have xxxi.

The Return from Parnassus. 4to. London. 1606.

Thirty days hath September,
April, June, and November,
February eight-and-twenty all alone,
And all the rest have thirty-one;
Unless that leap year doth combine,
And give to February twenty-nine.

*Lines used by John Ball, to encourage the Rebels in Wat
Tyler's Rebellion. Hume's History of England,*
Vol. I. Chap. 17. Note i.

When Adam dolve, and Eve span,
Who was then the gentleman?

---

* See Butler's Hudibras, *ante*, p. 119.

*From the Garland, a Collection of Poems, 1721, by Mr.
Br—st, author of a Copy of Verses called
"The British Beauties."*

Praise undeserved is Satire in disguise.*

THOMAS A KEMPIS — (1380-1471)

Man proposes, but God disposes.**
Imitation of Christ. Book i. Chapter 19.

And when he is out of sight, quickly also is he out of
mind. Book i. Chapter 23.

Of two evils, the less is always to be chosen.
Book iii. Chapter 12.

FRANCIS RABELAIS — (1483-1553)

Translated by Urquhart and Motteux

To return to our muttons. Book i. Chapter 1. Note 2.
To drink no more than a sponge. Book i. Chapter 5.
Appetite comes with eating, says Angeston.
He looked a gift horse in the mouth. Book i. Chapter xi.
By robbing Peter he paid Paul, . . . and hoped to catch
larks if ever the heavens should fall.
He did make of necessity virtue.
I 'll go his halves. Book iv. Chapter 23.
The Devil was sick, the Devil a monk would be;
The Devil was well, the Devil a monk was he.
Book iv. Chapter 24.

MIGUEL DE CERVANTES — (1547-1616)

Don Quixote. Translated by Jarvis

Every one is the son of his own works.

Part i. Book iv. Ch. 20.
I would do what I pleased, and doing what I pleased,

---

* This line is quoted by Pope, in the 1st Epistle of Horace,
Book ii., —

"Praise undeserved is *Scandal* in disguise."

** This expression is of much greater antiquity; it appears in the
Chronicle of Battel Abbey, from 1066 to 1176, page 27, Lower's
Translation, and also in Piers Ploughman's Vision, line 13994.

I should have my will, and having my will, I should be contented; and when one is contented, there is no more to be desired; and when there is no more to be desired, there is an end of it. Part i. Book iv. Ch. 23.

Every one is as God made him, and oftentimes a great deal worse. Part ii. Book i. Ch. 4.

Blessings on him who invented sleep, the mantle that covers all human thoughts. Part ii. Book iv. Ch. 16.

SIR PHILIP SIDNEY — (1554-1586)

The Defence of Poesy

He cometh unto you with a tale which holdeth children from play, and old men from the chimney-corner.

I never heard the old song of Percy and Douglass, that I found not my heart moved more than with a trumpet.

There is no man suddenly either excellently good, or extremely evil.

They are never alone that are accompanied with noble thoughts. *Arcadia*. Book i.

THOMAS HOBBES — (1588-1679)

For words are wise men's counters, they do but reckon by them; but they are the money of fools.
The Leviathan. Part i. Chap. 4.

FRANCIS BACON — (1561-1626)

He that hath a wife and children hath given hostages to fortune, for they are impediments to great enterprises, either of virtue or mischief.
Essay viii. *Of Marriage and Single Life*

Some books are to be tasted, others to be swallowed, and some few to be chewed and digested.

Reading maketh a full man, conference a ready man, and writing an exact man.

Histories make men wise, poets witty; the mathematics, subtle; natural philosophy, deep, moral, grave; logic and rhetoric, able to contend. Essay 1. *Of Studies.*

JOHN MILTON. — (1608-1674)

Tract on Education

In those vernal seasons of the year, when the air is calm and pleasant, it were an injury and a sullenness against Nature not to go out and see her riches, and partake in her rejoicing with heaven and earth.

The Reason of Church Government urged against Prelaty. Introduction to Book 2.

A poet soaring in the high reason of his fancy, with his garland and singing robes about him.

Beholding the bright countenance of truth in the quiet and still air of delightful studies.

Areopagitica

Methinks I see in my mind a noble and puissant nation rousing herself like a strong man after sleep, and shaking her invincible locks; methinks I see her as an eagle mewing her mighty youth, and kindling her undazzled eyes at the full midday beam.

Apology for Smectymmius

He who would not be frustrate of his hope to write well hereafter in laudable things, ought himself to be a true poem.

THOMAS FULLER — (1608-1661)

Holy State. Book ii. Ch. 20. *The Good Sea-captain*
But our captain counts the image of God, nevertheless his image cut in ebony, as if done in ivory.

Their heads sometimes so little, that there is no more room for wit; sometimes so long, that there is no wit for so much room.   Book iii. Ch. 12. *Of Natural Fools.*

They that marry ancient people merely in expectation to bury them, hang themselves in hope that one will come and cut the halter.   Book iii. Ch. 22. *Of Marriage.*

Often the cockloft is empty, in those which Nature hath built many stories high.   *Andronicus. Ad. fin.* 1.

ANDREW FLETCHER OF SALTOUN — (1653-1716)

*From a Letter to the Marquis of Montrose, the Earl
of Rothes, &c.*

I knew a very wise man that believed that, if a man were
permitted to make all the ballads, he need not care who
should make the laws of a nation.

HENRY ST. JOHN, VISCOUNT
BOLINGBROKE — (1672-1751)

I have read somewhere or other, in Dionysius Halicar-
nassus, I think, that History is Philosophy teaching by ex-
amples.   *On the Study and Use of History.* Letter 2.

BENJAMIN FRANKLIN — (1706-1790)

Poor Richard

God helps them that help themselves.

Dost thou love life, then do not squander time, for that
is the stuff life is made of.

> Early to bed, and early to rise,
> Makes a man healthy, wealthy, and wise.

Three removes are as bad as a fire.

> Vessels large may venture more,
> But little boats should keep near shore.

You pay too much for your whistle.

*From a Letter to Miss Georgiana Shipley, on the
Loss of her American Squirrel*

> Here Skugg
> Lies snug,
> As a bug
> In a rug.

LAURENCE STERNE — (1713-1768)

Go, poor devil, get thee gone; why should I hurt thee?
This world surely is wide enough to hold both thee and me.
Tristram Shandy. Vol. ii. Chapter xii.

Great wits jump.*   Vol. iii. Chapter ix.

Our armies swore terribly in Flanders, cried my uncle Toby, — but nothing to this.   Vol. iii. Chapter xi.

And the recording angel, as he wrote it down, dropped a tear upon the word and blotted it out for ever.

Vol. vi. Chapter viii.

SENTIMENTAL JOURNEY

"They order," said I, "this matter better in France." Page 1.

In the Street. Calais

I pity the man who can travel from Dan to Beersheba, and cry, 'T is all barren.

The Passport. The Hotel at Paris

Disguise thyself as thou wilt, still, Slavery, said I, still thou art a bitter draught.

Maria

God tempers the wind to the shorn lamb.**

THOMAS PAINE — (1737-1809)

Letter to the Addressers

And the final event to himself (Mr. Burke) has been that, as he rose like a rocket, he fell like the stick.

The Crisis. No. 1

These are the times that try men's souls.

Age of Reason. Part ii. ad. fin. (note).

The sublime and the ridiculous are so often so nearly related, that it is difficult to class them separately. One step above the sublime makes the ridiculous, and one step above the ridiculous makes the sublime again.***

---

* "Good witts will jumpe."
Dr. Cougham, Camden Soc. Pub., p. 20.

** "Dieu mesure le vent à la brebis tondue."—*Henri Estienne, Prémices,* etc., p. 47, a collection of proverbs, published in 1594.

*** Probably the original of Napoleon's celebrated mot, "Du sublime au ridicule il n'y a qu'un pas."

DON JOSEPH PALAFOX — (1780-1843)

Wart to the knife.   *At the Siege of Saragossa.*

THOMAS B. MACAULAY

Edinburgh Review, Oct., 1840, *on Ranke's History*
of the Popes.

She (the Roman Catholic Church) may still exist in undiminished vigor, when some traveller from New Zealand shall, in the midst of a vast solitude, take his stand on a broken arch of London Bridge to sketch the ruins of St. Paul's.

JOHN RANDOLPH — (1773-1833)

A wise and masterly inactivity.   *Speeches,* 1828.

WASHINGTON IRVING

The Almighty Dollar.   *The Creole Village.*

FRANCIS DUC DE ROCHEFOUCAULD — (1613-1680)
Maxim ccxvii.

Hypocrisy is a sort of homage that vice pays to virtue.

JOSEPH FOUCHE — (1763-1820)

It was worse than a crime, it was a blunder.

MISCELLANEOUS

"The blood of the martyrs is the seed of the Church."

"Plures efficimur, quoties metimur a vobis; semen est sanguis Christianorum."   *Tertullian. Apologet.,* c. 50.

"Corporations have no souls."

"They (Corporations) cannot commit trespass nor be outlawed nor excommunicate, for they have no souls." — *Lord Coke's Reports,* Part x. p. 32.

"A Rowland for an Oliver."

"These were two of the most famous in the list of Charlemagne's twelve peers; and their exploits are rendered so ridiculously and equally extravagant by the old romancers, that from thence arose that saying amongst our plain and sensible ancestors of giving one a 'Rowland for his Oliver,' to signify the matching one incredible lie with another." Warburton.

"It is unseasonable and unwholesome in all months that have not an R in their name to eat an oyster." — *Butler's Dyet's Dry Dinner.* 1599.

"Hobson's Choice."

"Tobias Hobson was the first man in England that let out hackney horses. — When a man came for a horse, he was led into the stable, where there was a great choice, but he obliged him to take the horse which stood next to the stable door; so that every customer was alike well served according to his chance, from whence it became a proverb, when what ought to be your election was forced upon you, to say 'Hobson's Choice.' " — *Spectator,* No. 509.